Why wo[uld] ... with her?

"I...don't know who you are or why you think you know me." Stella met the man's gaze, determined to prove her point, but somewhere deep inside, in the far recesses of her mind, something intangible registered.

A wild and primitive awareness flickered in his eyes, something predatory, an almost hungry look, as if she'd not only met him, but that he'd known her intimately.

As quickly as the moment came, it fled, and she was thrust back into the depths of lost time.

"This isn't funny, Stella." Luke stalked toward her, stopped and gritted his teeth. "I've been searching for you ever since you ran out on our wedding night."

Stella gasped, perspiration beading her lip. Wedding night? What was he talking about? She'd never been married....

Had she?

RITA HERRON

VOWS OF VENGEANCE

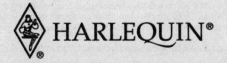

HARLEQUIN®

TORONTO • NEW YORK • LONDON
AMSTERDAM • PARIS • SYDNEY • HAMBURG
STOCKHOLM • ATHENS • TOKYO • MILAN • MADRID
PRAGUE • WARSAW • BUDAPEST • AUCKLAND

To all the fans of my Nighthawk Island series—
thanks for your feedback and support.
Hope you enjoy this one!

ISBN 0-373-22892-9

VOWS OF VENGEANCE

Copyright © 2006 by Rita B. Herron

All rights reserved. Except for use in any review, the reproduction or
utilization of this work in whole or in part in any form by any electronic,
mechanical or other means, now known or hereafter invented, including
xerography, photocopying and recording, or in any information storage
or retrieval system, is forbidden without the written permission of the
publisher, Harlequin Enterprises Limited, 225 Duncan Mill Road,
Don Mills, Ontario, Canada M3B 3K9.

All characters in this book have no existence outside the imagination of
the author and have no relation whatsoever to anyone bearing the same
name or names. They are not even distantly inspired by any individual
known or unknown to the author, and all incidents are pure invention.

This edition published by arrangement with Harlequin Books S.A.

® and TM are trademarks of the publisher. Trademarks indicated with
® are registered in the United States Patent and Trademark Office, the
Canadian Trade Marks Office and in other countries.

www.eHarlequin.com

Printed in U.S.A.

ABOUT THE AUTHOR

Award-winning author Rita Herron wrote her first book when she was twelve, but didn't think real people grew up to be writers. Now she writes so she doesn't have to get a *real* job. A former kindergarten teacher and workshop leader, she traded her storytelling for kids for romance, and writes romantic comedies and romantic suspense. She lives in Georgia with her own romantic hero and three kids. She loves to hear from readers, so please write her at P.O. Box 921225, Norcross, GA 30092-1225, or visit her Web site at www.ritaherron.com.

Books by Rita Herron

HARLEQUIN INTRIGUE
486—SEND ME A HERO
523—HER EYEWITNESS
556—FORGOTTEN LULLABY
601—SAVING HIS SON
660—SILENT SURRENDER†
689—MEMORIES OF MEGAN†
710—THE CRADLE MISSION†
741—A WARRIOR'S MISSION
755—UNDERCOVER AVENGER†
790—MIDNIGHT DISCLOSURES†
810—THE MAN FROM FALCON RIDGE
861—MYSTERIOUS CIRCUMSTANCES†
892—VOWS OF VENGEANCE†

†Nighthawk Island

CAST OF CHARACTERS

Special Agent Luke Devlin—An FBI agent who never crossed the line—until he met the enigmatic Stella Segall and married her.

Stella Segall—Luke's wife disappeared on their wedding night without a trace. Now, accused of murder, she insists she has no memory of her traumatic past or the man who claims to be her husband—Luke Devlin.

Dorothy Segall—Stella's mother supposedly sold her when she was an infant, but Stella's returning memories hint at a different story.

Kat Dixon & Jaycee Short—Two hired and trained killers just like Stella—or are they?

Spencer Grossman—Luke's superior at the agency suspected that Luke's partner was a bad agent. Now he's gunning to find out if Luke had joined him.

J. T. Osborne—Osborne's death was ruled a suicide—wasn't it?

Drake Sutton—A stranger who claims to be Stella's guardian—his sinister secrets may destroy them all.

Marvin Andrews—This reporter who will do anything for a story—will he die trying to write it?

The Master—He trained them all to kill without a conscience—is it his turn to die now?

Prologue

It was Luke Devlin's wedding day. The happiest day of his life.

Nothing could go wrong.

He and Stella had arrived at the chapel just before it had closed. They'd already exchanged vows. And now his wife was waiting in the honeymoon suite, preparing for their wedding night.

A night of ecstasy he couldn't wait to begin.

Neon lights flashed across the night sky on the Vegas strip as he rushed to the car to retrieve the champagne and roses he'd bought for the occasion. Granted, he wasn't much of a romantic. Hell, he wasn't romantic at all. And he wasn't even sure he knew *how* to be a husband. But he'd decided to give it a try.

After all, he'd never met anyone like Stella.

She hadn't wanted a big, fancy wedding and neither had he. She'd insisted they drive to Vegas, instead of marrying in D.C. where they'd met. They'd gotten in around eleven, picked out simple wedding bands at a jewelry store nearby and had a nice quiet romantic dinner with a bottle of red wine. After toasting their future, they'd found an Elvis chapel offering a special deal for midnight ceremonies.

Even though the chapel had been somewhat cheesy, he wanted the honeymoon night to be special. Memorable.

And it would be. After the ceremony, they'd hurried back to the hotel as excited as if they'd floated into paradise.

Heady images drifted to mind as he jogged to the elevator. Stella in a bubble bath waiting for him, sipping champagne as he licked bubbles from her breasts. Stella naked and lying on that heartshaped bed with her hair spilling across the pillow and her legs open wide. Stella whispering that she wanted to go down on him as they'd left the chapel. Him doing the same for her afterward, giving her pleasure, and hearing her long-winded ecstatic cries.

Then being inside her, all night long…

A blissful evening of making love where, for once in his life, he could forget he was FBI. That he had an endless number of cases to work. Murders to solve. Killers to hunt down. Women and children to protect.

A life of violent and heinous crimes.

One that didn't include pleasure.

A life he wanted to share with Stella.

A frisson of anxiety suddenly assaulted him, the hairs on the back of his neck prickling. He had this feeling often. Every damn time he went to a potential crime scene.

But not now.

Hell no. Not on his wedding night.

Exhaling slowly, he exited the elevator, cut his gaze

up and down the hallway, then toward the intersection where the halls met. Nothing seemed out of place. No strangers were lurking in the corner. No guns pointed his way.

Still, his pulse accelerated as he approached his room and inserted the key in the door. The wooden panel swung open.

Maybe Stella had left the door unlocked. Maybe she was waiting in the room, naked with strawberries and whipped cream on her belly. With chocolate sauce on her thighs, and promises in her eyes.

But that eerie premonition clutched at his chest again, and he felt for his gun, removed it from his jacket and slipped inside the room. All was quiet.

Eerily quiet.

Stella was nowhere to be seen.

He glanced at the bathroom but heard nothing. Only a daunting silence. As if the air couldn't move. As if death had taken residence inside.

His gaze flew to the bed. On top of it lay the white sundress Stella had worn to the chapel. Blood dotted the skirt. The spaghetti straps looked as if they'd been torn.

Shock and horror momentarily paralyzed him. What the hell was going on?

He rushed to examine the damaged dress, picked it up and sniffed the blood to make certain it was real. A mental image of Stella wearing it down the aisle flashed in his head. The bodice had stretched tight over her breasts, the scalloped skirt swirling around her slender bare legs.

His throat closed, confusion and fear clawing at him. Where was she?

He scanned the room in search of a clue. Her white

stilettos were underneath the bed as if she'd kicked them off. The bouquet of fresh flowers had been crushed. Tossed on the end table.

And her suitcase was missing.

Instincts honed by years of training kicked in. He angled himself sideways and approached the bathroom, his imagination going wild. Other images flashed before his eyes. Stella on the floor bleeding. In the tub, drowned. Stella with her neck sliced open. Her eyes staring into space in death.

He'd seen it all before. The horrors of mankind.

But God, not on his wedding night. Not to his bride.

His lungs tightened as he peeked through the door. But no one was inside. The shower stall was closed. She might be hiding behind it.

So might an attacker.

Inching through the doorway, he poised his gun, ready to fire, then jerked open the door.

But it was just as empty as the room. Only a bottle of Stella's raspberry scented shampoo lay on the floor, the contents spilling over, the red color floating in puddles like blood.

Something bad had happened to Stella.

He flew back to the room, scanned it one more time. A piece of hotel stationery was crumpled on the floor as if it had fluttered there when he'd opened the door.

A ransom note? A Dear John goodbye?

One ear cocked for sounds of an intruder, he leaned over and read the note.

"Don't come after me. Goodbye."

The writing was shaky. The note scribbled. A drop of blood dotted the white.

Had she decided their marriage was a mistake, or had she met with foul play?

Rational thoughts kicked in. If she had left of her own accord, why would there be blood?

He grabbed the phone, called security, identified himself as FBI, then ordered them to get someone up to his room. Within minutes, a chunky man with rumpled clothing and a name tag that read Ted appeared.

Ted frowned as he entered. "You reported that your wife is missing?"

Luke nodded, and removed a photo, the only one he had. The wedding photo of them kissing at the chapel. Thunderous emotions rose in his throat at the sight.

In the photo Stella had clung to him. She had looked happy. She had wanted to marry him and be his wife.

"We'll call the local police." Ted cocked a brow. "But, sir, are you sure she didn't just, er…" He cleared his throat and glanced away, his face turning red. "Leave you?"

"There's blood on her dress," Luke snapped. His emotions pinged back and forth between fear and panic. And there was more. He had wanted to make a life with Stella. Had finally carved a place in his heart for a woman. Now it felt as if someone had jammed a knife in his aorta, and his own blood was spurting out.

It was unbelievable. Luke Devlin was an agent, a hardass, a man who investigated cases for others. He'd never been personally involved in a case before. That is, except for his partner J.T.'s recent death.

The man glanced at the dress, then at Luke and took a step back. A wary look darkened his eyes.

Luke looked down and realized he'd made a fatal

mistake. He'd touched the dress. It held the scent of his cologne. His dirty handprints muddied the white.

And his fingerprints were all over the room. His day had gone from bad to horrible to worse. He was the husband, the one who'd called in the crime.

When the police came, they'd treat him as a suspect. As if they thought he'd killed his wife.

Just as they'd treated him after J.T.'s recent demise.

Chapter One

The sheets were soaked in blood.

Stella stared at them in shock, then glanced down at her trembling hands. More blood. On her hands. Her fingers. Her nightgown.

It was still wet.

Then she saw the man.

Moonlight streaked his face, a golden outline of his still form stark against the bloodstained sheets. Nausea rose to her throat, the room swirling.

He was lying beside her. Half naked. Brown hair. Average features.

Except blood oozed from his mouth. And his chest had turned crimson, a red stain spreading across his torso.

The stench of body odors assaulted her, and a scream bubbled in her throat. She scrambled backward off the bed, panic clawing at her. Her foot hit a gun and sent it skittering to the floor. She jerked it up, turning it over in horror as she realized the man had been shot with it.

Her heart pounded as she glanced back at him again. Whoever he was, maybe he was still alive.

But he wasn't breathing. His eyes were wide open, glued to the ceiling in the cold shock of death.

Suddenly the door burst open, and a policeman raced in, his weapon drawn. Stella froze.

The officer took one look at the dead man, then her, and his ruddy face went white. "Don't move, ma'am."

Her hand shook violently, the gun bobbing up and down as she realized how the scenario appeared. "I—"

"Put the gun down," he barked.

"But I…I don't understand."

His tone hardened. "Now. Slowly lower the weapon to the floor."

Shock and fear washed over her as she did as he instructed.

"Raise your hands in the air."

She swallowed hard, then lifted her hands in surrender as he trained his gun on her. It was obvious that he thought she'd killed the man in the bed.

Only she had no idea what had happened.

LUKE DEVLIN'S phone trilled, the sound cutting into the silence of the night as if announcing trouble. He reached for it, one foot already sliding off the side of the bed, his mind playing the guessing game as to the nature of the call. A new case. An old one. Somebody else found dead. Something mysterious happening at Nighthawk Island. More bioengineering related to terrorism and chemical warfare. Their newest undercover plot—or maybe the feds with information on who had killed his partner J.T. Osborne last year and made it look like a suicide.

Or something about his wife's disappearance.

He scrubbed a hand over his face, wishing he'd had at least an hour or two's worth of sleep. But sleep eluded him these days. So he welcomed work to relieve the pain and restlessness. "Special Agent Devlin."

"Devlin, this is Lieutenant Rawlins of the Savannah Police Department."

"Yes?"

"I just got a call from one of my officers, Detective Black. They found your wife."

His heart thundered in his chest. Stella had been found. Alive?

Time vaulted to a standstill. For the past year, he'd searched endlessly. Even as a suspect himself, he'd pushed the cops and feds for the truth. They thought he'd crossed the line on this one.

But Luke Devlin never crossed the line. Not for anyone. Just as he didn't believe that J.T. had been corrupt, either.

Eventually clues had turned up that made them believe Stella had left of her own accord. That she was alive and well, moving from one place to another. That she didn't want to be reunited with him or to be found. But her disappearance had stamped a black mark on his career. Too many questions left unanswered. Too much doubt and suspicion for anyone to completely trust him.

Especially after all the trouble with J.T.

Although the police had officially deemed his partner's death a suicide, and had called off the search for Stella, Luke hadn't given up.

He had to solve the mystery around J.T.'s death. He'd been undercover at CIRP, getting close to finding out their latest experiments when he'd died. Luke needed to know what had happened to his wife on their honeymoon.

"Devlin?"

Luke cleared his throat, collecting himself. "Where is she?"

"Sunset Motel."

"What?" His hand tightened around the phone. Was this some kind of joke? "What's going on?"

"You can meet Detective Adam Black when you get there," Lieutenant Rawlins said.

The officer started to hang up, but Luke needed more information. "Wait. Just tell me—is she … alive?"

A long hesitation stretched over the line, riddled with tension. Heat from the open window brushed his neck, and he broke out in a cold sweat.

"Yes, but, Devlin, there's something else you need to know." Rawlins paused, the scent of death and fear filled Luke again.

"What?"

"She's going to be charged with murder."

The breath whooshed from Luke's chest. Moving on instincts so natural, he didn't contemplate his actions, he closed the phone, yanked on his jeans, grabbed a shirt and jogged to his car. His mind raced while he cut through the streets of Savannah. Though it was midnight, tourists crowded the streets, Saturday night partiers in full swing. Booze and music floated through the humid summer air from River Street, a cruise ship had docked in town creating more chaos in the summer atmosphere. The roar of a siren in the distance reminded him that crimes had been at an all-time-high for the area, the closing of the bizarre suicide cases a while back having added more hype to the mysterious happenings at Nighthawk Island.

Questions rattled through his head, the same ones that had haunted him the past year. Where *had* Stella been all this time? Why had she left him on their wedding night? Had their marriage been some kind of scam? Had she been ill and decided not to burden him? Had she decided that she couldn't stay married to him, that he was some kind of cold, FBI agent who didn't know how to treat a wife? Or had she been in some kind of trouble, something she was afraid to confess to him?

But if she'd left of her own free will, why had there been blood on her wedding dress? That one element had bothered him, kept him searching for her, kept him awake each night with disturbing dreams and images.

And if she had been in trouble, why hadn't she attempted to contact him sometime during the last year?

He maneuvered around traffic and a handful of pedestrians leaving a blues bar, then sped onto the road leading to the motel, leaving the historic side of Savannah with its town squares, haunted cemeteries and classy bed-and-breakfasts behind. He continued on, threading his way to the outskirts, to a rinky-dink motel that catered to low-rent patrons and truckers, ones who didn't mind bug-infested rooms and two-bit hookers.

What was Stella doing at a place of this caliber? And why had Rawlins said they were going to arrest her for murder? Had she been held captive? Had she become involved with another man and gotten in over her head?

He approached the motel room with a mixture of

trepidation and excitement. Finally he'd glean some answers. Learn the truth. Get closure.

Look into her eyes and know why she'd put him through hell the last year. Why she hadn't loved him enough to stay around.

The blue lights of the Savannah police car swirled through the darkness, the neon lights of the Sunset Motel blinking as he parked. One letter was missing in the word Sunset so it read the Sunet, and the building was so dilapidated it should have been condemned. A smattering of rattletrap cars filled the lot, a group of spectators already hovered in the parking lot, smoking cigarettes and mumbling, obviously aware their peaceful night had been interrupted by crime.

He barreled his sedan into a parking spot, killed the engine, then grabbed his badge and flashed it at the locals working to secure the scene.

"Special Agent Devlin."

The squatty officer at the bottom of the steps spoke first. "Detective Black said you'd be here."

Luke nodded, grimacing. The man obviously knew about his past. As Luke climbed the steps to the second floor, he dodged a reporter and cameraman. The motel rooms were lined up, each with its own outdoor access to the balcony. The doors were painted an avocado-green that had faded to a pea-green color from the blistering sun and relentless summer heat.

Seconds later, he stopped at the doorway, his gaze skimming past the security guard talking to one of the local cops. Through the open doorway, he cataloged details of the scene.

Blood was splattered everywhere, soaking the sheets

and dotting the stained gray carpet. The foul odors of death hit him. The mumblings of policemen at work. A crime scene crew that had just arrived.

He saw Detective Black inside, then his gaze landed on Stella, and his heart literally seemed to stop beating.

She sat stone-stiff in one of the motel chairs, her hands knotted, her normally olive complexion a pasty-white, while Black questioned her. Luke hadn't imagined the gut-wrenching reality of seeing her alive, in the flesh.

The hair that had been buttery-blond was now jet-black, not short and layered as when he'd known her, but a long tangle of ebony waves that sent a bolt of surprise through him. Surprise and sexual desire. He had wanted Stella the first moment he'd met her. The moment he'd looked into her pale green eyes.

She'd been leaning against a bar wearing a red dress that hugged her curves and a pair of rhinestone earrings that had dangled down to her shoulders. Although surrounded by gaping men, she'd appeared disinterested. Instead she'd looked lost and lonely.

After the death of his partner and the questions surrounding J.T.'s final days, Luke had been vulnerable himself. He'd always admired the way Osborne had juggled his career and a wife, and for the first time in his life, Luke had wanted the same.

In an uncharacteristic move, he'd bought Stella a drink. Three vodka martinis later, and they'd crawled into bed for some of the steamiest sex in his life. Stella had completely poleaxed him with her odd mixture of shy vulnerability and her bold lack of inhibitions about her body.

A month later, they'd eloped and that blissful month of premarriage heaven had turned into the year from hell.

He cleared this throat, struggled for calm and entered the room. An eerie quiet descended as if the black cloud that had been following him had swallowed the light. Two officers parted, their stares burning his back as he walked toward her. They knew who he was. Knew this was his wife.

When he stopped, only a breath away from her, he expected recognition. He waited, bracing himself, tamping down his anger.

She looked up, and he stared into her light green eyes, was caught anew by the sensuality and sweetness he'd once seen there. A bruise darkened her cheek, though, and a cold look of horror filled those crystalline eyes, as well as a dead emptiness that shook him to the core.

Yes, it was Stella.

But not the Stella he remembered.

She didn't speak, jump up and greet him, or offer an explanation. Didn't acknowledge that she was his wife. Didn't move to touch him, to hold him or beg him for forgiveness.

He had to clear his throat twice to make it work. "Stella?"

He waited, his lungs tight.

"Yes." An odd, almost distant look glazed her expression, then her voice came out in a low whisper. "Who are you?"

STELLA'S HEAD was swimming. First from waking up to find the dead man beside her, her hands coated in blood. Then the security guard and police with their questions and accusing eyes.

And now this stranger…was staring at her, calling her name, looking at her as if he'd seen a ghost.

As if she should know him.

"Come on, Stella," he said in a harsh voice. "It may have been over a year since we were together, but don't pretend you don't recognize me."

"I…" She gripped her hands in her lap, shuddering at the blood on her fingers. The sticky dark substance had seeped beneath her fingernails, soaked into her skin, settled in the fine lines on her palms. The smell suffocated her, the feel of the dried blood caking her hands nauseating her.

She desperately wanted to shower and rid her body of the stench of the dead man, but the detective beside her had already informed her bathing was impossible. They had to collect evidence. Fingerprints, DNA. Protect the crime scene.

So they could nail her for the murder.

Even though confusion muddled her mind, she knew what they were thinking. Realized she looked guilty. For God's sake, she'd been holding the gun when the cop had arrived.

And what had this man said—that it had been a year since she'd seen him? Denial swept through her. If she'd ever met him, she wouldn't have forgotten him. He was too powerful. Virile. Sexy. Intimidating.

Then again, she couldn't remember anything except her name.

"Stella?"

She studied his features, searching for familiarity, for

any dot of a memory to return. His tight jeans accentu-
ated the massive power of his body. He was tall, over
six feet, broad-shouldered and muscular. His eyes were
dark, too, like two hot coals on fire, probing, unnerving as if he never smiled. A broad jaw brushed with dark
stubble gave him a sexy appearance, but the tight set to
that jaw indicated he was angry.

Why would this man be angry with her?

"I…don't know who you are or why you think you
know me." She met his gaze, determined to prove her
point, but somewhere deep inside, in the far recesses of
her mind, something intangible registered.

A wild and primitive awareness flickered in his eyes,
something predatory, an almost hungry look, as if she'd
not only met him, but he'd known her intimately.

As quickly as the moment came, it fled, and she was
thrust back into the depths of lost time.

"This isn't funny, Stella." The man stalked toward
her, stopped and gritted his teeth. "I've been searching
for you ever since you ran out on our wedding night."

Stella gasped, perspiration beading her lip. Wedding
night? What was he talking about? She'd never been
married….

Had she?

LUKE STUDIED his wife's reaction, his temper battling
with other emotions he didn't want to admit. He was
glad to see her. Relieved she was alive. Furious that
she'd left him.

And he ached to hold her. To grab her, drag her into
his arms and tell her how terrified he'd been that she
was hurt, in trouble, needing him. How he'd nearly

been out of his mind the last twelve months. That he'd imagined horrid scenarios, seen her face in death a thousand times in his mind, her neck twisted or broken, her body covered in blood with glazed eyes.

That he'd made love to her a thousand times in his mind.

Stella stretched her left hand in front of her. "You must have me confused with someone else, mister. I've never been married."

His dark eyebrow shot up. "Stop lying," he said in an icy tone. "I'm not in the mood to play games and neither are these other officers." His cold gaze slid across her, sideways to the bed where the dead man lay in a pool of blood, then back to her hands. "Who was *he?* Your lover?"

Detective Black cleared his throat. "Devlin, maybe you'd better let me handle this."

Luke glared at him. "What has she told you so far?"

Stella knotted her hands and glanced at the detective as if he were her friend. As if she thought she needed protection from *him.*

"I don't know who this man is," Stella said to Black. "Or what he's talking about. Do I have family to call?"

"You told me you had no family." Luke swallowed, grappling for control. After all Stella had put him through, how could she pretend she didn't recognize him?

Detective Black gestured for Luke to step aside. Reluctantly he did so, well aware Stella tracked his movements.

"I think she may have amnesia or be suffering from shock," Detective Black said. "I want the paramedics to evaluate her."

Luke nodded. "All right, but just to cover our asses. She's lying through her pretty, white teeth."

Black shrugged. "Then see what you can get out of her. So far, I've hit a dead end. She insists she doesn't remember anything except her name, that she doesn't know the victim."

Luke grunted. Hell, maybe she hadn't known him, maybe she'd picked up a stranger for a one-night stand. "She was in bed with the damn man."

Not how he'd expected to find her. He'd be a laughingstock all over the bureau. Disgust rode through him in waves. He'd made a fool of himself the last year. Begging the feds to keep looking for her and trying to clear himself at the same time.

Dammit, he'd chased down lead after lead. Tortured himself over what might have happened to her. Blamed himself for not protecting her. Nearly lost his damn career.

And now here she sat, denying their marriage ever existed, pretending not to know his name…

Fury raged through him as he turned back to her. She was trembling and had shrunken back into the chair as if the cheap flimsy plastic might save her. Hating the sympathy that struck him, he stifled the urge to grab a blanket and wrap it around her arms, to calm her.

Instead he steeled his voice. "All right, Stella. Tell me what's going on."

Her eyes smoldered with unease. "Like I told the police, I don't remember what happened. I woke up around midnight and found this man in my bed. B-blood was everywhere." Her face paled as she picked at the dark stain between her fingers.

"Go on."

She bit down on her lower lip. "I…had blood on me, then I scrambled off the bed and saw the gun."

"You were holding it when the security guard arrived."

"I…I picked it up off the floor. I…" She gestured toward the bed. "I …don't know this dead man, though…or what's going on. I…swear it. I don't even remember checking into the motel."

"What is the last thing you remember?"

Stella glanced away, rubbed at her temple as if a headache brewed. "Nothing."

A muscle tightened in his jaw, his agent instincts battling with the memory of her in his arms. He almost believed her. Almost.

Too much circumstantial evidence pointed to the opposite.

He knelt and touched her hands, ignoring the stab of desire the movement cost him. She was shaking, her eyes glued to the crimson stains on her fingers and nails.

He slowly turned her hands over, and saw the powder burns.

Powder burns didn't lie. Only people did.

"STELLA'S OUT of control." He poured himself a glass of brandy from the bar in Sutton's office, swirled it in circles, then downed it in one swooping gulp. While he waited on Sutton's response, he savored the taste for a moment, the slow burn of the alcohol sliding down his throat and warming his belly.

"I have the situation in hand," Sutton barked. "She told the police nothing."

"You lost her a long time ago, Sutton. You should have disposed of her when she first betrayed you and attempted to escape."

"My plan will work. Just be patient."

"Patient? Devlin won't let go. And we've put too much into this project for you to go soft."

"Soft?" Sutton's voice rose. "If I'd gone soft, how the hell did I pull off what I just did? My plan is a stroke of genius."

He tapped his nails on the smooth marble bar. "What if it doesn't work? You're taking a chance just letting her near the cops. And that bastard Devlin—he's no fool." He paused and poured himself another drink. "He didn't let the hype about his partner being corrupt deter him."

"It did for a while. He got sidetracked with Stella."

"You think we can use her to do the same now?"

"It's worth a shot."

He harrumphed. Sutton might think he had things under control, but that was near impossible now. Stella was like a pipe bomb—unpredictable. "Know that I'm monitoring your ever movement, Sutton. If Devlin gets too close, if Stella starts remembering and talking, then I'll kill them both."

"I understand."

Did he really? Sutton might be riding the line, but *he* wasn't. He was the same ruthless man he'd been trained to be. He took without mercy. Trained the others to do the same. And he hadn't gone soft.

Soft meant forgetting what he had learned from the Master. The Master who had led him down the path years ago, just as he continued to lead the others.

Stella had been one of them. One of the hardest to break. One of the ones who'd tried to get away.

But there was no escape. Only a price to pay for trying to do so.

And Stella would learn just how high that price could be.

Death for her lover. For herself.

But first…first, she would know the pain of betrayal.

And if Sutton couldn't handle it, he'd meet death himself.

Chapter Two

Luke's gaze rose from Stella's bloodstained, powder-burned fingers to her heart-shaped face. The bruise stood out, stark now, making his gut clench.

As their gazes locked, the undeniable spark of sexual energy that had zapped him the first time he'd met her rippled through him again, as strong and potent as before. The pull of those green eyes, luminous with fear and confusion, tugged at emotions he refused to acknowledge.

Sweat beaded on his forehead and hands, and his heart pounded. The air was sultry, the room cloying with the stench of death, yet she still had the power to touch some unreachable place that he hadn't even known existed. A weak place that wanted and needed her in spite of the fact that she had deceived him.

Every protective instinct he'd ever possessed reared itself, taunting him with what-ifs.

What if Stella were telling the truth? What if she were innocent? What if this were some bizarre case that was more complicated than a wife having skipped out on her husband? What if the dead man had tried to hurt her, and she'd been acting in self-defense?

What if she hadn't wanted to leave you?

Hopeful, stupid thoughts that no jaded cop or federal agent was supposed to think, much less allow himself to believe. Not even for a second.

After all, he'd seen the worst of mankind, witnessed deplorable acts and betrayals that had destroyed his trust in the human soul. And years ago, he'd steeled himself against falling for a wounded woman.

Until Stella had stepped into his life.

Then a part of him had gone soft.

He hated softness of any kind. Had been trained not to tolerate it.

He glanced at her hands again, registered the absence of her wedding ring, and he won the war with his primal instincts. Humiliation and anger raging inside him, he wiped the sweat from his brow and spun away from her, leaving her to face the cops alone while he spoke with the crime scene unit. The medical examiner, Dr. Yates, studied the body, making notes. A sandy-haired man in his twenties and a red-headed female CSI tech were collecting evidence, combing for fingerprints, picking hair fibers from the bed and carpet, lifting prints from the water and wineglasses on the end table. The sheets were soaked, hanging askew, the white pillowcase marred with a crimson stain in the shape of a hand. Stella's hand.

Luke swept his gaze over the victim. Noticed not for the first time that he was naked. He had brown hair, was average height, no distinguishing marks on his face, except for a scar by his right ear. He was lying on his back, his legs partially dangling over the side as if he'd tried to get up and run. One hand was thrown over his head, the other on his chest where the bullets had pierced his heart. His body was lean, but not muscular. Hairy. And his jewels... They were limp, hanging in plain sight.

Not a man he'd have thought Stella would have been attracted to.

Luke's hands knotted by his sides. Had Stella slept with the man, then killed him? And if so, why hadn't she tried to cover up the murder? Why had she screamed as if she was calling for help? She hadn't even attempted to hide the weapon.

Or maybe her amnesia act was part of her plan...a self-defense ploy to keep her from jail.

He scratched his chin, assessing the rest of the room with a trained eye. There were no suitcases. No bottle of wine to go with the wineglasses. No...clothing.

No woman's purse.

The pieces of the puzzle didn't fit. Where were the man's clothes?

He stalked to the bathroom and found one of the investigators bagging a pair of slacks, so he introduced himself to both the techs. "Any ID in there?"

"No. So far, we haven't found any for him or her," Doug, the male investigator, said.

"Condoms?" Luke gritted his teeth while he waited. The female, Jill, shook her head. "None in here."

"I didn't find any in the bedroom, either," Doug added.

Luke frowned. Stella had always insisted on condoms. So had he, for that matter.

Then again, maybe she and the dead man hadn't gotten to the nitty-gritty yet.

Luke rushed to the bedroom, checked the nightstand. Empty except for the motel Bible.

He closed the drawer with a scowl, then approached the body again, parking himself by the M.E. "What do we have so far?"

"It appears he died of multiple gunshot wounds. Two to the chest. Close range. My guess from the size of the wound, a .38."

The same kind of gun Stella had been holding.

"Any other injuries?"

Dr. Yates rolled the man to his side, indicating several bruises that marked his lower back. Others, less noticeable due to the blood on his chest, covered his torso. And another one darkened his thigh.

"Any signs that he had a weapon?" Luke asked.

"No powder burns on his hands. There is some blood under his fingernails. We'll send it to trace." The M.E. glanced up and frowned. "There are hair fibers that appear to match the woman's."

Luke spotted a long, black strand of hair caught in the man's finger and his stomach knotted. "Any evidence that indicates someone else might have been in the room?"

The crime scene techies returned. "We've found a few short brown hairs in the bathroom," the sandy-haired CSU guy reported. "They don't appear to belong to the victim or suspect."

Jill shot a look of disdain around the room. "Could be a product of a shoddy cleaning staff," she muttered. "You know they rent these rooms by the hour."

Luke nodded. "Bag and tag all of it. I want every inch searched, including the bathroom." He glanced back at Stella, bracing himself for his next move. "I'll arrange for a doctor to examine her, and make sure he goes over her body with a fine-toothed comb. He'll look for defensive wounds, signs of sexual activity, blood, semen, DNA from the victim and any other source."

"She's already asked to shower," Jill remarked, a hint of derisiveness in her tone. "At least she isn't screaming rape."

Luke aimed a frigid stare toward the tech. "This is a murder investigation, so let's stick with the evidence. Stella claims she has no memory. We don't know what happened, and until then, we can't rule out any possibility."

The woman's expression went from cocky to chastised in a flash.

He exhaled, then pivoted to study Stella again, to look for the lies and the truth in the woman he'd married. She was shaking violently now, had her arms wrapped around herself in a blatant attempt to hold herself together. Either that, or she was a consummate actress.

Still, her hair was disheveled, dried blood crusted her fingers and nightgown, and the pale skin of her legs was showing. His eyes narrowed. A long scar glistened along the bottom edge of the nightshirt—a scar that hadn't been there a year ago. And he would know. He'd loved, kissed and touched every inch of her.

"She can't clean up until she's thoroughly examined," he said, shutting out the memory. "And I'll inform the doc to examine that scar on her leg. I want to know how long it's been there and what caused it. Our psychiatrist will also conduct a complete neurological. Let's see if her amnesia is for real." He jerked his gaze back to the crime scene agents. "Get me the results from here as soon as all of you are finished."

He strode toward Stella just as Detective Black snapped the handcuffs on her delicate wrists.

STELLA GLANCED UP at the federal agent, Luke Devlin, the handcuffs rubbing heavily against her skin as the detective gripped her shoulder to lead her from the room. For a brief second, she thought something flickered in the man's enigmatic eyes—a look that hinted at an apology. Or maybe a promise that he would help her. That she wasn't alone in the world of darkness that had become her life.

But the feeling disappeared as if it had never existed, and tremors racked her body again, a trapped feeling overwhelming her. She had been trapped before. Had been held against her will. Made to do unspeakable things. And a man had been involved. A black-haired man with cold, black eyes.

Then she had tried to escape.

But there were harsh punishments for that.

Snatches of memories, all in black and white, blurred reality, and the room twirled and spun in a dizzying frenzy. She saw herself—running, running, running. But she could never escape. Never outrun the demons.

The detective cleared his throat. "Mrs. Devlin…are you all right?"

She blinked at the sound of the title, the agent's face wobbling back into focus along with the voices and murmurings of other officers. The stench of the dead man's body floated toward her, then the overwhelming scent of another man invaded her space—Luke Devlin.

He carried with him a commanding air, a mixture of a spicy, woodsy scent that simmered with sexuality, a scent that overrode the worst of the stench in the room.

Had she really married this stranger? And if so, why didn't his face look familiar?

She took one more look at the dead man's body on the bed and nausea rose to meet with the clogged air in her throat, renewing her panic. The man was dead. She had no idea who he was. Or who had murdered him.

But she was going to jail for the crime.

She would be locked behind bars, a prisoner...

Just as she had been before.

She balked and drew back, stiffening and digging in her heels. The men halted. Another officer reached for his gun as if preparing to fire if she attempted to escape.

"Relax. We're taking you to the hospital to be examined," Detective Black said in a low voice. "Agent Devlin is arranging for a CSI team to collect evidence and have you evaluated."

Luke Devlin approached her, closing his cell phone as he stopped by her side. He stood towering over her, a mass of muscle, black hair and intimidating eyes. "I'll escort her, Detective."

A mixture of unease and relief poured through her. If this man had married her, he must care about her. Surely he would help her figure out the truth. Help her regain her memory. Keep her from prison. But the rigid grip of his fingers as he half dragged her to the police car indicated differently.

Outside, she gulped, startling as thunder rent the air, and lightning zigzagged across the gray, mantled sky. It was pitch-black, not a star in sight.

She shifted and looked up at Luke Devlin. His eyes were the same eerie combination of black and gray.

This man might have claimed to be her husband, but would he really help her?

And what if the memory of being trapped meant she had been trapped by him...

THE VULNERABILITY in Stella's green eyes stole Luke's breath. When they'd stepped outside, panic had tightened her slender body.

She was scared.

Dammit, she should be. Every piece of circumstantial evidence so far pointed to the fact that she had murdered a man. Probably in cold blood. Maybe even premeditated.

And now she was hiding behind a smoke screen of amnesia.

How common was memory loss anyway?

They descended the steps, his instincts as an agent warring with a compassionate side he hadn't known he possessed. A side that no one else had ever touched.

But he had pledged vows to this woman. Promised to protect, honor and love her for the rest of their lives. As bitter and cold as he liked to believe he was, he was a man of his word.

They reached the car, and he opened the back door, then squared his shoulders, and helped her inside. Part of him wanted to drive her to some hideaway, a place where they could talk and be alone.

Someplace where he could have his damned unfinished wedding night. Maybe if he made love to her, she'd remember him. He sure as hell hadn't forgotten her touch. Or what her lips had done to his body. And how it felt to sink himself inside her.

Detective Fox, Adam Black's partner, jumped into the driver's seat while Luke claimed the passenger side. "To the hospital?" Fox asked.

Luke gave a clipped nod. "Yes."

A sound of distress rippled from Stella, but Luke ignored it and gestured for Fox to drive. Thunder barreled and rolled across the moonless sky, and rain began to pound the roof.

The ten-minute ride seemed like an hour. Fox was forced to a crawl from the heavy rainfall. Luke occupied himself by phoning the hospital to confirm that the doctor who worked for the police department was available to examine Stella. Fox parked in the emergency entrance, and angled himself toward Luke.

"You want me to wait?" Fox asked.

Luke shook his head. "No, I'll assume custody of her now."

Stella gave him a helpless, frightened look from the back, but he ignored it. Although when he climbed out, he shucked off his jacket and wrapped it around her arms to shield her from probing eyes as he coaxed her into the hospital. She halted in the entrance, her body trembling. He smoothed a damp strand of hair from her cheek in comfort, but she pulled away from him, as if he were the enemy.

"What's going to happen to me?" she asked in a low, shaky voice.

"They're going to examine you, take trace evidence. Make sure you're healthy enough to…"

"To be arrested?"

His gaze met hers. "This exam is as much for your safety and protection as it is for us, Stella. They might discover evidence that someone else was at the crime scene, too."

Or that she'd been assaulted and had defended herself. He latched onto the thought. As awful as that idea was, the other possibilities were more daunting.

She bit down on her lip, her tangled hair falling over her forehead and across her cheek. He was tempted to reach out and push it back again, but jammed his hand inside his pocket instead. He couldn't allow himself to touch her. The other officers would see what a complete and utter fool he'd been. Think he'd lost his edge and couldn't function on the case.

And he *had* to work this case.

Losing J.T. had made him look incompetent. And then falling under Stella's seduction...

Besides, touching her was too personal. It meant reviving memories he couldn't deal with right now. Rubbing salt into wounds that were so fresh he felt as if they'd just been sliced open. Tearing into layers of his heart that had been ripped away one time too many already.

Yes, he had to work this case. Prove he could handle it.

Because he had to know the identity of the dead man in Stella's bed, and his relationship to her.

And if she had killed him.

As THE DOCTOR escorted Stella back to the examining area, Luke Devlin stationed himself at the door like an armed guard, proving to Stella that there was no love lost between them.

Weak and drained, she mentally prepared herself for a different type of interrogation. But the minute Luke Devlin had deemed himself her police guardian and ordered these tests, she realized nothing could have prepared her for the humiliating ordeal of being treated as a suspect in a murder investigation.

The doctor, a middle-aged man named Morton, had icy hands that scraped, combed and touched virtually every inch of her. She felt violated in ways she hadn't known existed.

On the heels of those vile feelings, an uneasy realization swept through her—the familiarity of being treated like a subject instead of a person. That sudden premonition was as unsettling as the remainder of the exam, which she barely endured without screaming.

As soon as the physical torture ended, an Asian psychiatrist, Dr. Wong, put her through a battery of psychological tests and questions that proved to be even more exhausting.

By the time she finished, she wasn't just worried about her memory loss but her sanity. And she still hadn't been allowed to bathe. It was almost as if they were playing mind games, leaving the stench of blood and death on her, hoping to drive her to a confession.

"So you don't remember anything before you woke up in that hotel room, Stella?"

Thank heavens the woman had finally accepted that she didn't know how to respond to the title Mrs. Devlin. It simply was too foreign for Stella to believe that she'd been married and didn't remember a wedding or her husband.

It shocked her even more to know that she'd married

that cold, unnerving man who'd ridden up front in the police car with another officer while she'd suffered the inhumanity of being shoved in the back behind a cage like an animal. He hadn't spoken to her on the ride to the hospital, and had simply presented her to the doctor who worked with the forensic scientists and crime scene unit, as if he had no personal or emotional involvement with her.

Then again, maybe they hadn't had one. Maybe that's the reason she'd left. She'd been running from *him*.

Had he come looking for her? Had he cared what happened to her? Or had he simply viewed her departure in his calculating, unemotional way and said good riddance?

"Stella?"

She jerked back to the present, exhaustion weighing her down. She was incredibly thirsty, too, her mouth so dry her lips were sticking together.

"No, I told you I don't remember anything." She rubbed a weary hand over her forehead, then noticed the blood again and cringed. "When can I get a bath?"

"We're almost finished."

"How about a drink of water?" In spite of the heat outside, her teeth chattered. "And a blanket?"

For the first time since she'd arrived, Dr. Wong's expression softened. In response to her request, the doctor retrieved a pitcher of water from a sideboard, poured Stella a glass and handed it to her. She also grabbed a blanket from the closet and wrapped it around Stella's shoulders. Stella drank the water greedily, already craving more as she tugged the blanket tighter around her.

When she finished the second glass of water, Dr. Wong narrowed her eyes. "Have you been ill recently?"

"I…don't know. Why do you ask that?"

"Because you seem dehydrated. And you're pale, have faint bruises beneath your eyes."

A desperate sob rose in Stella's throat. "I'm just so tired."

"What's your full name?"

"Stella Segall…that's all I know."

"Where do you live?"

Stella searched her memory banks for some clue, some memory, anything to stir from the depths of despair threatening to swallow her. Finally she shook her head. "I don't remember."

"Do you have family?"

She shrugged, any patience she'd had dissipating. "Not according to Agent Devlin. And if I remembered one, don't you think I would have asked for them by now, called and begged them to get me out of this god-awful mess?" She raked her jagged bloody nails across the table. "Why? Did Agent Devlin lie to me? Has someone come forward looking for me? Do I have a mother, a sister or a brother maybe?"

Dr. Wong averted her gaze slightly, and Stella read the gesture as an answer. Luke Devlin hadn't lied.

He was the only person she had. And he had brought her here in handcuffs.

What a sad testament to her life. Why *didn't* she have friends? Family? What had happened to bring her to this point?

You're a murderer.

The voice whispered in the far recesses of her mind, taunting her.

Was she really such a horrible person?

Dr. Wong crossed her legs, her clipboard planted firmly on top of her black suit skirt. "Where have you been staying the past year?"

"I don't know!" Frustration exploded in Stella's voice. "Why do you keep asking me the same questions over and over? I told you I don't remember anything but waking up in that room and seeing the b-blood." She gulped, the images flashing again, sweat trickling down her neck and back.

"I'm hoping to spark your memory."

Stella gripped the water glass with trembling hands, the first glimmer of hope surfacing. "So you believe me?"

A long hesitation, followed by a labored sigh. "I believe something happened to you, something that you want to forget. Something traumatic."

Stella flinched. So the woman thought she was guilty.

Thought she'd repressed the facts. But how could she forget shooting someone? Or getting married.

And why had a stranger been in her bed instead of her husband?

Chapter Three

Luke met with Dr. Morton while the psychiatrist finished with Stella. "What did you find, Dr. Morton?"

"I haven't drawn any conclusions yet."

"Were there drugs in her system?"

"The blood tests should tell us that. I've sent everything to the crime lab."

"Did she have defensive marks?" Luke asked.

Dr. Morton hesitated, then consulted his notes. "Some, yes. There were skin particles under your wife's fingernails, bruises around her wrists and ankles, although some of them looked old."

"How old?"

"Months maybe."

"And that scar on her leg?"

"A knife wound of some kind. It's months old as well."

Luke swallowed. Perhaps she hadn't disappeared of her own free will. "So it's conceivable that she was attacked? That this man might have kidnapped her last year, and that he's been holding her captive since?"

"I can't make that conclusion. Although the bruises on her indicate she might have been assaulted or fought with someone recently, there was no evidence of sexual activity or rape."

Luke expelled a sigh of relief, uncertain whether that was good news or not. He sure as hell didn't want to hear that Stella had willingly slept with that man, or that the man had attempted rape. But an assault might help prove a self-defense case, and explain trauma severe enough to cause amnesia. Especially if the man had been holding her prisoner for months.

Dr. Morton shuffled his notes. "I'll let you know when the DNA results are in."

Luke shook his hand, thanked him, then headed to the psychiatrist's office. Down the hall, he spotted his superior, Spencer Grossman, standing beside Dr. Wong's office door. He was surprised to see Grossman here. For the past two years, he and the agent had clashed.

Grossman was a power hog, and played by his own set of rules. Basically, he was a real son of a bitch. And he had watched Luke like a hawk the past year, had threatened to suspend him more than once. Was that the reason he was here now? To pull Luke from the investigation?

The door opened, and Dr. Wong appeared with Stella by her side. The dried blood looked stark against her pale skin, fatigue lines drawing her slender features tight. She seemed impossibly small and fragile, as if she were a fine piece of glass that might shatter any second.

Odd, but when he'd first met her, he'd thought she was fragile, too. But she'd possessed a spunky side that had surprised him time and time again. Although he had suspected she'd had secrets she was trying to hide…

Secrets he'd looked forward to exploring. Secrets he should have uncovered *before* he married her.

"If she's through, the locals can take her to the precinct and book her," Grossman said.

Stella wavered slightly, glanced at the psychiatrist, then at him as if desperate for someone to save her from herself.

Luke ground his molars. "Let her clean up first."

Grossman grunted. "She can clean up at the jail *after* she's booked."

Stella shuddered, and Luke steeled himself against the sympathy tugging at him. But the image of Stella being forced to endure the humiliation of a prison shower before a night in jail sent a cramp through his already churning stomach.

He glared at Grossman. "She's cleaning up here."

"She's under arrest for murder," Grossman said. "And you don't belong on this case."

"She's also still part of an ongoing missing persons case, and she's obviously not well," Luke stated. "And you know I'm not leaving the case alone. Not after all this time."

"Watch it, Devlin. You're a hair away from losing your job."

Luke ignored the comment, although Grossman's threat was the very reason he had to stay and investigate. Before his career ended, he'd find out what happened to his partner and Stella. Although J.T.'s wife had thought that J.T. might have had an affair, Luke didn't believe it for a second. J.T.'s death had something to do with Nighthawk Island and the cloning project he was investigating, not a woman. In fact, Luke suspected that his partner's death wasn't a suicide, that he'd been murdered, and his death made to look like he'd killed himself. Unfortunately a suicidal death kept J.T.'s wife and son from collecting the insurance money owed them.

But Luke had no proof about the murder. He'd been looking into the theory that CIRP had killed J.T. because he was on the verge of discovering something about them. Then Luke had met Stella and gotten sidetracked.

Now, he had to know the truth about her, too. The two cases couldn't possibly be connected, could they?

No. Stella had met him in D.C. at a bar. She'd been flirty. Fun. Seductive. A break from the intensity of his job. They'd had a fling. Then he'd made her his wife. He'd vowed to love, honor and protect her.

He hadn't done so on his wedding night.

He sure as hell had to do so now.

STELLA WANTED TO HUG Luke Devlin for letting her shower at the hospital. Every inch of her reeked of blood and death, of being examined and touched by a strange man's hands. She scrubbed and scrubbed, lathering her body repeatedly, digging beneath her fingernails to scrape away the dried blood and remnants of whatever extraneous elements dirtied her skin. Her hair came next, soaking the long strands with the cheap hospital shampoo and scrubbing her scalp until it felt raw.

Minutes later, a knock sounded, intruding on her peace. She couldn't stall the inevitable. She was going to jail for murder.

And she had no one to call for help.

Worse, she couldn't even help herself.

Sighing, she towel-dried her body and hair, then slipped into the faded hospital scrubs the nurse had provided, grateful at least to be out of her soiled nightgown. She'd felt naked in the sheer fabric, as if every cop and doctor who'd looked at her had touched her bare skin with vile eyes. As if she'd come up lacking.

When she opened the door, Agent Devlin was standing to the side. The other agent, Grossman, stared down at her as if she were roadkill.

Another officer had also joined them, jangling a pair of handcuffs. Stella couldn't look at Devlin, simply resigned herself to her fate and allowed the officer to handcuff her and lead her back to the police car. Outside, a camera flashed, and she glanced up in horror to see a reporter jamming a microphone in her face.

"Is it true that you murdered the man at the Sunset Motel tonight? Who was he? Your lover?"

Luke Devlin shoved the reporter aside, raised his arm to shield her face from the camera flash again, urging her into the back of the car. She ducked her head, burying herself as low in the seat as possible as the siren's shrill sound rent the air, and they drove off into the night.

The next hour proved to be another ordeal in humiliation. The booking process, blatant stares of accusations and suspicion, fingerprinting, the photo that would go into a file. Finally a surreal numbness spread through her, a coping mechanism she guessed. By the time the guard escorted her to her cell, she almost collapsed.

But Luke Devlin appeared, then motioned for the

guard to leave them alone. She dropped onto the dingy cot, avoiding looking at the open toilet in the corner of the room and fighting nausea at the stench of urine and sweat permeating the cell. It was late so most of the other prisoners were asleep, although an off-key, sick humming radiated from the other side of the wall, and another inmate beat the concrete repeatedly, a testament to the dregs of society with which she was now housed.

Luke stood silently assessing her, his big body making her feel more crowded than she already did with the bars closing around her.

"Stella, are you all right?"

Unwanted tears pooled in her eyes. She didn't think she'd ever felt so helpless in her life. Still, she nodded, refusing to look at him and reveal her fear.

The mattress squeaked and dipped with his weight as he sat down beside her. She knotted her fingers together, plucking at the baggy prison suit she'd been forced to change into.

"I spoke with the doctors. Dr. Wong believes you've been traumatized and have repressed memories of the murder." He hesitated, his voice gruffer when he continued, "But what about me? What about last year—you must remember our wedding night."

She shook her head, a shiver running through her. He sounded upset, almost hurt…

With fingers of steel, he grabbed her arms and shook her. "What happened that night? Why did you run out on me?"

"I…don't know." Her voice broke, tears overflowing. "I'm sorry. I…wish I did."

His fingers dug into her flesh. "Think. You suggested

we elope. We drove to Vegas, you picked out the chapel, the ring—"

"When?" she whispered, gulping back tears. "When did we get married?"

His jaw flexed. "Thirteen months ago."

She frowned, searching her memory banks, but she couldn't recall ever going to Vegas. "How did we meet?"

He swallowed, his dark eyes raking over her. "In a bar in D.C. I bought you a drink, we talked…"

And had sex. She read it in the flare of heat in his eyes.

It had been good, too. No, not good. Hot, steamy. And they'd done it more than once.

That part she wanted to remember.

He certainly did.

"What happened?" she asked in a low voice. "After the chapel, what did we do?"

He chewed the inside of his cheek. "We went to a hotel. I ran to the car for champagne. When I got back to the room, you were gone."

A flash of some memory teetered on the edge of her consciousness, but she couldn't quite grasp it. If he'd gone out for champagne, then they must have been happy. So why had she left?

"I found a note telling me not to follow you. But there was blood on your wedding dress, so I was frantic." He paused, scrubbed a hand over the back of his neck. "Is that what you wanted? For me to run after you, to think you were hurt—"

"No." Panic squeezed her chest into a fireball. "I…have no idea what you're talking about. I…wish I did. I wish I remembered you."

"You lied to me back then, and you're lying now."

His voice hardened another notch. "After you disappeared, I checked you out. You told me you were a graphic designer, but when I investigated the company on your business card, no such company existed."

Stella searched his face, couldn't believe his words. "But why would I lie about my job?"

"That's what I've been waiting a year for you to tell me." Flames of anger spiked his voice again. "The police thought I had something to do with your disappearance. I almost lost my damn job because I was a suspect. We hunted for your body for months."

Stella shook her head in denial. "That can't be true." She stood, anger taking root. "*You're* lying to me now, trying to make me think I'm some horrible person. This is all part of your good-cop, bad-cop routine, isn't it? Break me down so I'll confess even if I don't remember what happened."

"I'm not playing games with you, Stella."

She was so confused. Her head throbbed, her palms were sweating. The world spun again, making her dizzy. "I don't know what to believe…"

"Believe this. We were married." Without warning, he jerked her to him, lowered his head and captured her mouth with his. The kiss was rough, erotic, full of pent-up emotion and anger. Steeped with blatant desire. His tongue probed inside her mouth, and he sucked and nipped at her lips, tasting, exploring, conjuring up sensations foreign to her, but so sultry she ached for more. Yearned for him to erase the horrors of the night with his touch.

He slowed his ministrations, and the kiss softened, turned tender. Erotic. So sweet that tears came to her eyes. She'd never been treated with gentleness or loving hands. That much she knew.

He seemed to remember what he was doing, where they were, and the kiss changed again. Anger and suspicion tainted the taste. Finally he jerked away, and she stumbled back onto the bed. He didn't bother to try to catch her.

Instead he turned and stalked to the cell door, yelled for the guard to unlock it, and stepped outside. For a long moment, he stood ramrod straight with his back to her, his chest heaving up and down. She pressed her fingers to her mouth, uncertain what to say. That she'd never been kissed like that. That she wished she did remember him, but that his face and touch were as foreign to her as the dead man in her bed had been.

That she wanted him to hold her and kiss her again. Make her remember what it had been like between them. Why she'd agreed to be his wife.

When he faced her, he met her gaze with a cold emptiness that splintered her desire. She recognized that kind of emptiness because she'd felt it so many times herself.

Still, hunger darkened his eyes, but the emotion was steeped in distrust and anger. He tossed a photograph into the cell. It fluttered to the floor, but her eyes followed it as it fell. The picture captured her and Luke kissing—in a wedding chapel.

So he hadn't been lying...

"I'll be back tomorrow for your arraignment," Luke said in a gruff voice.

His stony gaze cut over her one more time, then he walked away without a backward glance. She picked up the picture and stared at it, trying desperately to recall her forgotten wedding night as she collapsed onto the bed. But only blackness filled her mind. Weary and frightened, she hugged her knees to her chest and faced the dirty wall.

Finally the tears she'd struggled to suppress flowed from her eyes and splashed against the prison pillow.

LUKE STRODE THROUGH the double doors to the outside of the jail, and leaned one arm against the brick wall, his breathing rasping out as he inhaled the sultry summer air. Heat and humidity caused his clothes to stick to him, and the few cars on the road in the middle of the night spewed exhaust, adding to the cloying air.

Only it wasn't the sound of cars or late night partiers that disturbed him. It was his own idiotic behavior back there.

What the hell had he been doing?

Kissing a suspect? Kissing Stella…

As if the last thirteen months hadn't cost him enough, he'd had to relent to his raging need for her and his instinctual desire and kiss her.

Because she had been the angel of light that had obliterated the darkness after J.T.'s death.

But what had he been trying to prove today?

That he was so potently sexy that his kiss would miraculously cure her memory loss?

He'd heard Dr. Wong's report. The amnesia was real. She had been traumatized.

Did that trauma have something to do with her initial disappearance, or the events of the night before?

The station house doors opened, and two officers lumbered out, heading to their police-issued vehicles. He grabbed his composure like a lifeline, fished in his pocket for his keys and planted a mask over his emotions as he strode to his own car.

Ten minutes later, he parked at the small house he'd rented on Skidaway Island and climbed from the vehicle. The scent of the ocean drifted toward him, the gushing of waves against rocks mingling with the thunder. Another storm cloud opened up, sending down sheets of rain in a downpour. He jogged to his house, opened the door and hurried inside. A shot of bourbon warmed his icy blood as he booted up his computer and accessed the files he'd collected so far on his wife.

There was very little there. Mostly her lies.

Her name had been real. Her birth certificate filed. Her parents listed as dead.

The job had been bogus.

He'd chased her for a year and now found her just miles away from Nighthawk Island and the research facility he and the feds had been investigating. It had to be a coincidence.

Although he'd been in law enforcement too long not to take a second look. Coincidences just didn't fly.

Frustrated and exhausted, he scrubbed a hand over his hair. Who the hell was Stella Segall? And how had he been such a fool to fall for her?

She was nothing but a pack of lies.

And he had turned a blind eye, ignoring instincts, listening to his sexual drive instead of his common sense.

The kiss rose to taunt him. Her green eyes. The feel

of her naked skin against his. The memory of his sex inside her body.

Damn. It had been over a year, and her touch still haunted him. Her lips and hands had done incredible things to him. And she had moaned and cried out each time he'd slid inside her as if she'd never been loved by a man. As if *he* were her first time.

How could she have forgotten making love with him when the thought drove him completely wild?

An even more disturbing thought rattled his composure and shattered his male pride—had she been faking her reaction to him when they'd made love a year ago?

Had her cries of ecstasy been lies in disguise?

SOMEWHERE AROUND dawn, Stella finally fell asleep. But nightmares filled the dark hours, thrusting her back in time.

WHERE WAS her mother?

She was five years old. Terrified, she peeked around the bedroom at the other girls, all lined up on cots, huddled in the darkness. Their faces were barely visible from being scrunched beneath the covers.

Together. But alone.

No one talking. No one whispering. All too afraid to ask.

Was her mommy ever coming back to get her?

Or was she in another dark room, on a cot lined up with the other mothers, wondering when they could see their children?

She closed her eyes and tried her best to conjure her

mother's face. Sometimes Stella saw her in her dreams. But she'd been torn away from her so long ago that Stella had forgotten what her face looked like.

Had her mother forgotten her as well?

"You're not supposed to remember." The other girls' voices whispered in her mind. "They'll punish you if you do. You'd better keep quiet."

An image appeared to her then. A dream or a memory, she wasn't sure. An angel's face floated above her bed. Long blond hair. Green eyes. She reached for Stella with slender fingers.

"Stella…"

"I'm here, Mommy."

Seconds later, her mother's screams broke the night. "I want my baby back! Bring her to me! Please, don't take her away!"

But each time they shoved her mother away, dragged Stella deeper into the darkness. The unknown. She was alone. With no one to save her.

And when she asked, they claimed her mother had died.

But in her dreams, her mother was alive.

Were her dreams only wishful thinking?

Rolling to her side, Stella burrowed beneath the heavy quilts, hiding from the demons that came to snatch her at night.

They did things to her that she didn't want to think about. Things that weren't right. Things the other girls never talked about.

But she saw the horror in their eyes.

Saw them change. Become quiet. Obedient. Robot-like. Afraid to argue. Afraid to think. Afraid to cry.

So she hid and sobbed into the pillow, aching. Wondering why they locked them in this terrible room. Wondering if they would ever release them and let them go home.

If they had a home to go to.

She'd heard the girls' chatter when they thought no one was listening. Knew the rumors. That the parents were gone forever. That they hadn't wanted the girls anyway.

That soon she would forget, too. Then the hurt would stop. It was better that way, they said. Better to be numb. Not to care. Not to feel.

She saw that emptiness in the others. The light fading each day as if it had been snuffed out during the endlessly cold nights.

Suddenly a loud sound burst through the room. Metal and wood pelted her covers. Bianca and Nadine screamed. She peeked above the covers, and her eyes went wide.

A ball of fire rolled through the room, the orange flames licking the wooden-beamed ceiling and splintering it into pieces. She scrambled up, saw the chair beside Nadine's bed catch on fire. Nadine cried out and huddled toward the top of the bed, hugging her teddy bear.

Flames ripped along the wall, clawing at the curtains, eating the braided rug. Stella screamed, a shrill sound that sounded almost animallike. Then fire crawled up the side of her own bed, licking at her feet.

Suddenly he was there. The big man with black hair and black eyes.

Orange flames lit a halo around his evil face. "I'm here to save you. Come on, Stella. Just take my hand."

The fire singed her feet, picked at her toes, rippled up her legs. She had to escape. She couldn't just lie here and catch on fire.

So she took the man's hand. Let him lift her and carry her away.

He was the devil. She knew it. But she was all alone now.

And she'd do whatever she had to do to survive.

STELLA JERKED AWAKE, staring into the silence, willing the unknown to offer her answers to a past that was as lost as the child inside.

The evening before crashed back. The blood. The man with the dead eyes.

The other one, the one who claimed to be her husband. Luke Devlin. Kissing her goodbye.

He had given up on her. Left her here to rot just as the others had when she was little.

She'd trusted him once. She had no idea how she knew that, but in some deep corner of her mind she sensed it was true.

But he was as much the enemy now as the others.

BY EARLY MORNING, Luke arrived at the jail. He'd already arranged for Stella's court appearance, pulled some connections to have her released on bail in his custody. Then he could watch her like a hawk, arrange medical treatment for her, uncover the truth, help wake her memories from their deep sleep. Make sure she was all right.

How would she react when he told her she was coming home with him?

It didn't matter. After all, she had no family, no one else to turn to. And he wanted answers.

Although he hadn't slept a wink all night for contemplating what those answers might be.

Or that having her in his home might destroy his equilibrium.

The guard led him to her cell, and he sucked in a deep breath as he stopped and studied her. She was lying on her side in a fetal position, her body rocking slightly back and forth. His gut clenched. He had a strong feeling she hadn't slept, either.

As he approached, she rolled over to face him, and he had to swallow hard not to whisper a comforting word. Dark circles shadowed her pale green eyes which looked bloodshot and tearstained. Whatever fingernails she'd had left had been chewed down to even more jagged edges than before. And the bruises on her face, neck and arms looked even more harsh in the early-morning light.

But the disoriented expression clouding her face disturbed him the most. It was almost as if she were looking at him but couldn't see him. As if she'd slipped into a catatonic state to keep from dealing with the present.

He needed to consult with Dr. Wong again. See if she needed medication or to be hospitalized.

"Stella?"

She pushed herself up to a sitting position, no evidence of emotion dawning.

"It's time for your arraignment."

She stood and walked to the cell door, still in that surreal state, as if the night had incapacitated her. The guard unlocked the door, and Luke stepped to the side, then touched her arm gently. "Are you okay?"

For a fraction of a second, fear registered in her eyes. Without speaking, she nodded, the mask dropping over her emotions again as she fell into step beside him.

A half hour later, they'd maneuvered the motions of the arraignment, his concern for Stella mounting at the quiet intensity with which she absorbed the ordeal. Luke contemplated arguing his reasoning for assuming custody of Stella when the courtroom door burst open, and two men entered. Luke recognized one, Lamar Winslow, a high-powered attorney who had represented some major players in the political community.

The other man was tall, had black hair with gray at the temples, was dressed in a pin-striped suit, sported a Rolex that cost more than Luke's entire wardrobe, and possessed an arrogant air that immediately made Luke's suspicions skyrocket. Who the hell was he, and why was he here?

"Excuse me, Judge," Winslow said. "We're here representing Stella Segall."

The judge glanced down at his notes, then back up, studying the men over bifocals. "You're late, gentlemen. This proceeding is almost over."

"I apologize, Judge, but due to the late hour of the arrest, and the fact that I wasn't aware of this arraignment until a half hour ago, we made it here as fast as possible." Winslow moved forward with confidence as he gestured toward the other man who seated himself on the defendant's designated side. "This gentleman, Drake Sutton, was Stella Segall's legal guardian. He's concerned about her health and would like to post bail."

Luke swallowed, stunned. Stella had insisted she had no family. And when she'd disappeared, no one had come forward looking for her.

Beside him, Stella's eyes remained fixed on Sutton. The breath that whooshed from her lungs hinted at surprise, but in her eyes, recognition flared. She knew this man.

Another one of her lies. Luke tried to tamp down his frustration and anger.

Winslow produced papers to prove his point, and Luke clutched the desk edge with a white-knuckled grip.

"Your client is accused of murder, Mr. Winslow."

"We're aware of that, your honor, but she's also sustained injuries, is suffering from traumatic memory loss and needs medical care. I spoke with the doctor at the hospital where she was examined. She's dehydrated and needs bed rest."

"She can get that in jail," the district attorney cut in.

Winslow gave him a withering stare. "The psychologist also stated that the trauma of prison might worsen her mental condition. I can assure you that she isn't a flight risk. We'll be glad to see that her passport is turned over to the courts. Mr. Sutton will also submit his own if necessary."

Passport? Luke grimaced, once again feeling like a fool. Stella had claimed she'd never been out of the States. In some moronic romantic fantasy, he'd imagined taking her to Europe and showing her the world one day.

Oblivious to his turmoil, the judge quickly made his ruling. Winslow and Drake Sutton posted bail. Sutton rushed to Stella. She remained frozen in the hard wooden chair. Luke resigned himself to the fact that he'd lost this battle. Stella wouldn't go home with him. Instead she'd go to Sutton's place.

He approached Sutton anyway, unable to allow Stella to leave with this man without more information. "Mr. Sutton, I'm Luke Devlin, Stella's husband." He extended his hand, but Sutton simply stared at him instead of accepting the gesture.

"Where have you been the past year? We posted news reports on TV looking for Stella, but you didn't respond."

"I was out of the country most of the year," Sutton replied. "Out of touch."

"What kind of business are you in that keeps you away from the news?"

"I'm a serious art collector, and I dabble in numerous international businesses. Stella is an adult, but we still see each other fairly often."

Luke folded his arms. "You still didn't answer my question."

Sutton narrowed his eyes. "All right. I did see Stella this past year. She flew to Paris to meet me after your unfortunate marriage."

Stella frowned next to Sutton as if confused by their exchange.

"Stella decided the marriage had happened too hastily," Sutton added.

"Then why run?" Luke asked. "Why leave a bloody wedding gown on the bed?"

"Women are impetuous, who knows what goes through their minds sometimes?" Sutton offered a smarmy smile. "I'll instruct my attorney to draw up the necessary papers to dissolve the marriage immediately."

Luke glanced at the blank look on Stella's face. Still tormented by the hot nights he'd spent with her, he shook his head at Sutton's offer. "No. I refuse to sign anything until Stella recovers her memory and tells me herself that the marriage was a mistake."

Just the fact that Sutton was in such a rush to rid himself of Luke aroused his suspicions. Sutton might claim he cared about Stella, but Luke didn't trust the man.

And he sure as hell didn't intend to bow out of Stella's life now without some answers.

Chapter Four

Stella shuddered as she glanced from the attorney to Sutton to Luke to Devlin.

Who could she trust?

The tall, gray-haired man who claimed to be her guardian or the enigmatic stranger who insisted he was her husband? And he had the photo to prove it.

The fine hairs on the back of her neck prickled as Drake Sutton touched her arm. She glanced sideways at Luke Devlin, but fury radiated from every pore in his masculine body. Not even a hint of the erotic kiss they'd shared the night before was reflected back.

That kiss had kept her awake half the night.

Then the nightmares had set in.

"Stella, my God, baby, what happened?" Sutton attempted to pull her toward him, but she couldn't allow this stranger to fold her into his embrace. Granted he was good-looking, seemed well-educated, appeared to care for her, and he had just offered a large sum of money as well as his passport to free her on bail, but he presented as much a mystery as Luke and everyone else in the room.

"Mr. Sutton…thank you for what you just did, but I… I'm afraid I don't remember you, either."

His eyes flickered with disappointment. "Oh, honey, the doctor was right. You need medical care." He extracted his wallet, removed a couple of photos and handed them to her. "Look, this is the two of us right after your parents died when you came to live with me."

Stella searched her memory banks. In the picture, she was just a small child. She stood beside a ten-foot Christmas tree that glistened with white lights. An enormous wreath hung over an ornately carved white mantel that had been strung with festive garland and berries. Several colorfully wrapped presents were piled beneath the tree, all artfully arranged with coordinating gift paper. The setting almost seemed…staged, as if it were fake, as if the decorations had been part of a photo set.

On some level the scene seemed familiar, though, but not in a good way. In a way that said she'd been upset that day. Maybe scared.

"I don't look very happy," she said, testing him.

Luke moved an inch closer, and Stella thought she felt a protective hand go to her waist. But when she glanced up, Luke stared down at her, not a shred of emotion on his face.

"You weren't, Stella," Sutton said with a shake of his head. "You were only five, and you'd just lost your folks. Your entire world was ripped apart. It was a difficult adjustment for both of us at first, but we managed." His look softened. "We even grew close over the years."

Stella wet her dry mouth with her tongue. "Do I have any brothers or sisters?"

Sutton hesitated slightly. "No, it was just you."

"What happened to her parents?" Luke asked.

"A boating accident off the coast," Sutton said. "They got caught in a storm…"

An image of thunderous waves swirling above her flashed into Stella's mind, but in the next second, the image seemed foreign. As if the idea of her parents boating wasn't possible.

And what about the dream where her mother had been crying out for her, the one she'd had the night before? Had that only been a nightmare, or could part of it have been real?

In the dream there had been a raging fire, not crashing waves.

"Was I with my parents when they died?"

Sutton shook his head. "No, thank God. The sailboat was completely demolished. You wouldn't have survived if you'd been in the boat." He gestured for her to look at the second photo. She studied the snapshot, trying to imagine beyond the picture to her past. In the photo, she was much younger, maybe seventeen. She and Sutton stood, arms linked, beneath a sprawling live oak with Spanish moss dripping to the ground. A huge castle-type Southern mansion was set back in the woods, a black wrought-iron gate encompassing the estate. It seemed cold, austere, cut off from the beauty of Savannah.

"That's my… our home," Sutton said in a low voice. "Where you grew up."

A protest teetered on her lips. Instead of looking homey, the estate reminded her of a prison. But after spending the night in a cell, she reined in those thoughts. Any place was more inviting than prison.

Of the two choices she had, going home with Drake Sutton seemed safer than leaving with Luke Devlin. After all, Sutton claimed to care for her like family, to want to help her get well. He wouldn't have the same expectations as Luke.

Luke might expect her to assume wifely duties, something she wasn't prepared to do. Although her body had sung with excitement when he'd kissed her the night before, on an instinctual level, she didn't think she was the kind of girl to sleep around. Then again, what did she really know about herself?

Luke had claimed they'd met at a bar—so she had jumped into bed with him the first night they'd met.

Then shortly after, she'd insisted they elope to Vegas…An uneasy feeling settled in the pit of her stomach. Just what kind of woman would dive into a relationship that quickly?

The type to have sex with strangers and forget them?

The type to commit murder?

LUKE'S INSTINCTS warned him not to trust Sutton.

Of course, his instincts had been completely off-kilter with Stella. Because his libido had entered the picture.

He was fighting the same problem again now, the urge to hustle Stella away to a private hideaway where he could take care of her, let her heal, and jog her memories. But he couldn't relent to his roller coaster emotions.

Not without some answers.

Sutton reached for Stella's arm to escort her from the now empty courtroom, and she angled her head toward Luke. "I…what's going to happen now, Mr. Devlin?"

"It's Luke." He swallowed hard. "The police will gather evidence, discuss the case. I'll investigate. We'll find out what happened."

"Will I have to go to trial?"

He wanted to soothe her fears, but he refused to lie. "That all depends on what the D.A. and your defense attorney decide to do." He grimaced. "If the D.A. has a solid case and no other suspects, they might offer a deal. If not, they'll set the court date soon."

Sutton cleared his throat and met Luke's gaze head-on. "We're not accepting a deal," Sutton declared. He stroked Stella's arm, his voice softening. "Don't worry, Stella. We'll clear you of this whole mess. All you have to do is go home with me, rest and recover. I'll take care of everything else."

Luke fisted his hands by his sides. "I'll need your address and phone number, Mr. Sutton. And I'm going to question Stella again."

Sutton removed a business card from his pocket and handed it to Luke. The card verified Sutton's assertion that he was an international art dealer. A home and cell number were listed, so Luke pocketed the card. He'd look into the authenticity of Sutton's businesses later.

And he intended to check on Stella daily.

"That's fine," Sutton said. "Now come on, Stella. I've arranged a private nurse to supervise your care."

Stella gave Luke an odd look, almost panicked, as Sutton coaxed her toward the door. Luke's chest tightened. Sutton's comment had upset her. Was she frightened of the man?

He followed Stella and Sutton out the door, half expecting, half hoping she'd turn back to him for help. But she didn't.

At the last minute though, she darted another brief glance toward him as they exited the building.

Luke squared his shoulders. "Stella, wait."

Damn, the heat was getting to him. That and the scared look in her eyes. He scribbled his personal number on his business card, then pushed it toward her. "Take this. If you need to talk to me, for any reason, just phone. Day or night."

Sutton reached for the card, but Luke wrapped Stella's fingers around it with his own hand instead. Her gaze met his, and emotions flickered in the depths, emotions he didn't want to analyze.

Sutton clutched her arm by the elbow, ushering her away to a dark Mercedes. Luke frowned and wiped the sweat from his brow. Damn, he sensed he'd just let Stella down somehow. That the man who'd pretended to be her savior was the big bad wolf in disguise.

His cell phone vibrated inside his jacket. He switched it off vibrator mode, then answered. "Special Agent Devlin."

"Agent Devlin, this is Marvin Andrews. We need to meet."

"I'm pretty busy right now, Mr. Andrews, so why would I want to take time to meet you?" Luke asked.

"Because of your wife."

The two words hung in the air between them, mired with unanswered questions.

"What do you have to do with my wife?"

A slight hesitation followed. "I might have some useful information about her."

"Who in the hell are you?"

"A reporter. I work for the *Sun*."

"Son of a bitch," Luke muttered. All he needed was the paper interfering with a federal investigation. And why would this guy have Stella's case on his radar?

"I don't have time for games, Andrews," Luke snarled. "If you have information, then spill it."

"That isn't the way it works. I want an exclusive on Stella Segall. The whole story."

Irritation crawled up Luke's spine. "What do you mean?"

"Just meet me and I'll explain."

"Tell me over the damn phone."

"That's not possible," the reporter hissed. "I have something you need to see."

Luke checked his watch then sighed. "What time and where?"

"Tonight. Midnight. The pier."

"How will I recognize you?"

"You won't. But I'll know you."

Luke snapped the phone shut, frustrated. He hated these clandestine meetings. But if there was a possibility the man had a lead on Stella's disappearance the past year, or why she'd lied to him in the beginning, he had to follow through.

Until then, he had some investigating to do on his own. Sutton was not the man he claimed to be.

He just had to prove it and figure out what Sutton wanted with Stella.

STELLA REMAINED silent on the drive to Drake Sutton's estate, her body knotted with tension. She wanted to understand the man who'd claimed to be her family, but he seemed reticent, almost angry.

Unable to bear the silence any longer, she finally gathered her courage and asked, "Do you know what happened to me the last year?"

His slid his gaze toward her, his expression schooled. "No."

"But you knew that I'd married Luke Devlin?"

His eyebrow shot up slowly. "You really don't remember?" He hesitated. "I thought the amnesia might be an act. A clever one, I might add."

"It's not an act. I seem to have forgotten my entire life." She scrutinized his features. "You didn't answer my question. Did you know I'd married Luke?"

"Yes. Like I said, you told me you wanted out."

"When I met you in Paris?"

He dragged his gaze back to the road and nodded.

"Do you know where I was living? Anything about how I wound up with that man in the hotel?"

His finger tap danced across the steering wheel as if he were trying to decide how to answer. Finally he sighed. "I don't have all the answers for you right now, baby. You need to stop pushing it. You're overtired."

"How can I not push it?" Stella screeched. "I'm facing murder charges."

He reached across the seat, patted her hand in a gesture that felt condescending. "I told you not to worry. I'll take care of things." His voice lowered an octave. "Let's get you home to rest. We'll talk more later. Then I'll fill in the blanks."

Exhausted, she finally relented, closed her eyes and let the lull of the Mercedes's engine relax her. When she opened her eyes again, palm trees floated past, the iron gates to Sutton's estate opened up and welcomed them inside. Sutton drove down a mile long drive lined with oaks, the feeling that she was disappearing into some kind of guarded compound not lost on her as the isolation of the landscape swallowed them.

The house that had seemed large in the photo loomed like a concrete monastery. Sutton parked in the circular driveway in front and cut the engine. Huge columns flanked the doorway. The sight of granite soldier statues on the brick stoop drew her eye. She checked to see if they represented a particular era or a famous American war figure, but saw nothing to denote their significance.

Still wary, she reached for the doorknob, but a short man with white hair appeared and opened it for her.

"Welcome back, Miss Segall."

Stella shivered at the sound of his deep voice, and struggled to place his face, but it was as unfamiliar as the brick pathway that led to the ominous-looking house.

Seconds later, she stood inside, her gaze scanning the art adorning the two-story foyer. Oil paintings covered the walls and marble statues stood on pedestals paying homage to the winding staircase—she wasn't a dealer or art connoisseur but each of the pieces looked pricey.

"They are originals," Sutton boasted, his chest puffing up with pride. "You always did admire them."

Stella gulped as the door shut behind her.

"Come on, Stella, I'll show you to your quarters. The cook will send up a tray. I'm sure you'll want to get a hot bath and rest for a while."

Fatigue tightened her shoulders. "That would be nice." She followed him up the marble stairs, then down a long hallway to a suite that had been closed off by a locked door. She frowned as Sutton withdrew a key, unlocked it, then gestured for her to enter.

"I'll have the nurse check on you shortly as well."

The mention of a nurse resurrected memories of the night before, of feeling violated. And somewhere in the far recesses of her mind, it tugged at another memory. Something even more painful…

"The entire wing is yours, Stella. You should have everything you need here."

She glanced up and thought she detected an almost evil note in his eye. With one hand, he opened the door to a sterile-looking bedroom. On second glance, it felt like a hospital room. The decor was monochromatic—white. The metal bed glimmered against the stark light. The room was void of decoration, color and personal items.

That thought alone sent her heart pounding just as it had when Sutton had first mentioned a nurse back at the courthouse. Other than the previous night, why would having a nurse bother her? Had she been ill as a child? Had an accident of some kind? Spent an extended time in a hospital?

And if she'd really lived here, where were her personal possessions? There wasn't a photo, a magazine, a tube of lipstick, not one item in sight that told her anything about herself.

He turned to leave and she shivered, uneasy at being left alone. Seconds later, the sound of a door being locked down the hall intensified her anxiety. She sank onto the bed, weak-kneed and nauseated, an enervated feeling engulfing her.

She'd just left one prison for another.

IT WAS LATE evening already, and the sun had faded, the night looming ahead, long and filled with mounting questions. Luke had spent the past few hours searching the FBI database for information on Drake Sutton but had found zilch.

Zilch as in no incriminating evidence or a connection to CIRP and Nighthawk Island.

Everything about the man had checked out so far. According to his sources, Sutton was well-known in the international art world, was a financial tycoon, dabbled in several stocks and international businesses, and didn't have so much as a parking ticket.

That itself had raised Luke's suspicions another notch.

No one who'd reached middle age had an unblemished past. Sutton was too good to be true. Too perfect.

Which meant he was a fake.

Unfortunately he was the most difficult kind to catch. The type who covered his tracks. Rarely made mistakes.

Rarely.

But everyone had an Achilles' heel and Luke would find Sutton's.

Maybe Sutton's was Stella herself.

Luke had seen the possessive way the man watched her, a look that hadn't been parental.

He didn't like the setup one damn bit. Stella was his wife.

He muttered a curse, dragged his hand over his face and strode outside for fresh air.

What the hell was he saying? Stella had married

him, but she'd brought a pack of lies with her, and had left him holding the bag.

And now she was back, in trouble, needing his help, and he had no idea whether to rescue her, or return her to jail.

His emotions didn't make any more sense than Stella's actions the year before.

He glanced at the sky, as if the heavens held answers, but darkness greeted him instead. The storm clouds still lingered from the night before, the gray-cast sky obliterating the stars. Ocean waves rocked in the background, beating against the shore, mimicking the roaring of his heart.

It would be another lonely night. One without answers.

Unless that reporter had a real lead for him.

Exhilarated at the thought, he strode back inside, grabbed his keys and decided to head down to the pier. He'd arrive early, grab a bite to eat at the marina, scope out the place, make sure he wasn't walking into some kind of setup. God knows he'd done that before and nearly ended up dead.

A few minutes later he managed to squeeze onto a bar stool, order a burger and wolf it down with a soda. Although he craved a cold beer, he needed a clear head tonight, his instincts alert. He sipped on coffee while studying the crowd. Since becoming an agent, he looked at everyone, every situation, with suspicion.

Except he'd thrown it to the wind the night he'd met Stella.

Had she really been that good in bed?

His sex hardened and throbbed, telling him yes.

Annoyed, he forced the image of a naked Stella from his head, although his body protested.

An hour later, he paid his bill and stalked into the humid summer night. A few late-night strollers walked hand in hand along the pier, and a teenage couple necked in the corner like star-crossed lovers who had escaped into their own romantic world for the night. A gray-haired woman pushed a baby stroller, probably babysitting tonight, and another couple laughed as their toddler dripped ice cream from a cone all over his chubby hands. Beyond them, toward the far end of the dock, two fishermen baited up and cast their lines while a stray dog wandered up and down the wooden plank searching for crumbs the seagulls might have missed.

So far, nothing appeared out of place.

A half-dozen teenagers arrived, one rapping to a headset, two girls giggling and chatting, and a skateboarder nearly ran him over, then had the nerve to curse at him.

Luke barely controlled the urge to draw his badge. To tell the kids to go home where it was safe, where they belonged.

Instead he shrugged off the incident, walked to the end of the pier and parked himself on a wooden bench in front of a catamaran tied to the dock. From that vantage point, he could see anyone coming. If there was one thing Luke couldn't stand, it was for someone to sneak up and get the jump on him—the way Stella had.

The minutes ticked by, the visitors dwindling, the air growing thicker with tension as Luke waited. The wind picked up, accentuating the smell of saltwater. By twelve-fifteen, the area was nearly deserted, but he continually scanned the dock in search of trouble.

A half hour later, he was just about to call it a night when someone climbed from the deck of a houseboat three slips down.

He sat up straighter, his hand automatically checking his weapon as the man approached.

Andrews, he assumed. He was hunched over, dressed in a ratty overcoat, looked like a homeless man. If this man was the reporter, why was he in disguise?

"Devlin?"

He stopped a few feet away, nudging a piece of popcorn through the crack in the pier.

Luke nodded. "Are you Andrews?"

The man gave a short nod, then dropped down beside him, a wine bottle in his hand. He tipped up the cheap wine, playing the part as he slumped lower in the seat.

Devlin frowned. "Why all the cloak and dagger?"

"You'll understand when you see what I have." The man discreetly fished a manila envelope from inside the raincoat and slid it onto the bench between them.

Luke flipped open the envelope, then removed several photos. They were all pictures of Stella. Stella wearing a slinky black cocktail dress sidled up to a tall, blond man at some kind of fancy dinner party. Stella in a dark room, pawing through what appeared to be a mahogany desk. Stella dressed in a wig, glancing across the street, then a follow-up shot of her ducking into a nearby dark sedan with a tall, austere man. "What the hell are these?"

"Photos of your wife. They look suspicious, don't they?"

Luke refused to take the bait. "I'm well aware my wife had a life before me."

"Look at the dates stamped on the back from the photo processor."

Luke's hands felt sweaty as he flipped them over. The pictures were all dated the last year.

So, she hadn't exactly been gagged and tied for the past thirteen months.

He cut his gaze back to Andrews, stone-faced. "Okay, I'll bite. What do you know about these?"

Andrews shrugged. "I have reason to believe that your wife is engaged in espionage, Agent Devlin."

Luke stared at the man in shock. "What are you talking about?"

"My sources tell me that Stella Segall is a covert agent. She's not working for our side." He hesitated, took another swig of the wine, then wiped his mouth with the back of his hand.

Luke didn't speak, couldn't. His mind was racing.

"Your wife didn't meet you by chance, Devlin," Andrews continued. "Your affair, the marriage—she staged it all. She's been using you the entire time."

Chapter Five

"Don't fight it, Stella. Give in to the darkness. Accept your fate. You have no control."

She rose slowly, submitting totally to the constant sound of the man's deep voice as he urged her to follow his commands. It was too hard to fight him. Impossible. He was the leader. The Master. And she had to bend to his will.

It had always been that way. As it had with the others. There was no escape.

Trying meant danger. Pain. Total darkness.

"That's right, Stella. You were born for this. Born to walk this path.

"Born to kill."

"No…"

The faint whisper of her denial sounded pathetic in the dank air that swirled between them. Had she dared deny him?

"Yes, Stella. You were born for this." He extended his hand, and metal glittered in the darkness. She felt the weight of it in her palm as she took the gun and checked to see if it was loaded.

As he'd instructed her, she slid the .38 into her

pocket, then walked to the other room. The man was waiting. Half-naked and sated this time. Hoping for more. Ready to take her to oblivion, if just for a few moments of pleasure.

The sheet slid down to reveal his bare chest, dusted in dark hair, then lower. She sucked in a sharp breath as she followed the trail to the heaven waiting below. Part of her ached and throbbed to ride that road again. To go the distance.

"Do it now, Stella," the voice ordered.

She nodded, a tear trickling from her eye as she raised the weapon and fired.

His body jerked back in response, his eyes flared open in shock. Blood splattered the pristine white sheets and sprayed the walls and pillows.

She began to shake all over. The horror of what she'd done. The voices that wouldn't leave her alone. The commands that would never end.

One voice promised that she'd belong to him forever. That she'd succumb to his beck and call.

The other promised to rescue her from it all.

But he'd failed in the end. And she'd been forced to kill him.

Now, she would never be free....

STELLA JERKED AWAKE, panting for air, a sob catching in her throat. Dear God, why had she dreamed something so horrible? That she was a killer...

Shadows flickered off the milky-white walls. She tensed, searching the room for an intruder. For the voice. The man.

But the sterile, white room was empty. No blood colored the walls or sheet.

Except in her mind.

And her memory.

The night in the motel…had she been remembering something?

No, she hadn't killed that man. She wouldn't believe it.

Besides, the man in the dream wasn't the one she was accused of killing. It was Luke Devlin.

The scent of antiseptic and cleaner assaulted her. Dizziness swept over her. The isolation must be wearing on her nerves. Making her dream unspeakable things. Things that she was incapable of.

Wasn't she?

She tried to sit up but slumped back down, exhausted. She'd been here three days. Each night had been filled with nightmares that she couldn't escape.

Her other dreams were equally disturbing. Although they didn't involve murder, they consisted of erotic moments with Luke Devlin. Of being touched and caressed, teased and loved until she cried out his name in ecstasy. Dreams of wanting the pleasure to last forever.

The reality of knowing that it wouldn't.

But each morning, she'd awaken, alone, to the fear and the emptiness. To the realization that serious trouble trailed her.

Matilda, the nurse Drake Sutton had hired, poked her head into the room and Stella quickly composed herself. If she complained of the nightmares, the nurse medicated her more. And Stella was beginning to think the medication stirred up more demons.

Matilda strutted in, looking slightly harried this morning. She was a pudgy, middle-aged woman and had been kind, but no nonsense. If Stella expected friendship or companionship, she'd have to ask someone else. Matilda assisted in arranging a decent diet for Stella, ordered vitamins and a sedative to help her rest, and dropped by regularly to take her vitals and monitor her recovery.

Other than that, she'd kept to herself.

"How are you feeling today?"

Stella shoved the tangled hair from her face. Her head felt fuzzy, the remnants of another dream from the night before echoing inside, making her skull throb.

She was in prison on death row. A guard had come to escort her to her death chamber. Her knees had given way, and he'd dragged her to a tiny, dark room, then strapped her down in preparation for the lethal injection.

"I just have to give you your injection." The nurse popped a hypodermic from her pocket, raised it and tapped the edge.

Stella jerked back and hugged the white comforter to her chest. She'd argued with Matilda about the shots the last two visits, insisting they made her more tired and lethargic, but Matilda had refused to listen, arguing that the doctor knew best, that rest might help her regain her memory.

But the injections and hours of drug-induced sleep only clouded her mind more.

She raised a hand to ward off Matilda. "Please, I'm better now. Not dehydrated or in pain at all. I don't need medication."

The nurse pursed her lips into a frown. "Don't be difficult, Stella. The doctor will cancel them when he thinks you're ready."

"But the drugs make me sleep too much. I…I need to start getting up, moving around, clear my head." Panic zinged through her as she fought a wave of claustrophobia. How long had she been here now? She'd thought it was three days, but it could be longer.

The hours and nights blended together. When she slept, she had nightmares. Or maybe she was remembering something else about her past. "I need to figure out what happened to me, Matilda. And I can't do that with these drugs in my system."

Matilda tsked in disapproval as if Stella were an obstinate child. "Mr. Sutton said to tell you he's taking care of everything."

Stella pushed back the covers and started to stand, but the woman suddenly moved in front of her. "Mr. Sutton has always protected you, Stella. You must cooperate if you wish for him to clear up this mess." She grabbed Stella's arm and jammed the shot into her flesh.

Stella flinched and stared at the nurse, for the first time recognizing a cold, calculating woman with a warning message in her eyes. Stella had best not fight the woman. If so, she wouldn't win.

The realization triggered a wave of nausea and renewed panic. She had to escape.

Where had she put that card Luke Devlin had given her?

The pocket in those prison clothes… She took a step

forward, glanced to the side in search of them. Maybe they were in with the dirty clothes. But where? In the bathroom...

No, Matilda had changed her gown each day, had carted each item of clothing away.

"Matilda, my clothes—"

"Lie back down, Miss Segall," Matilda said coldly. "You're going to hurt yourself."

The room grew fuzzy. A fog floated in front of her eyes. Stella had to find that card. Call Luke. Figure out the reason Sutton was keeping her locked inside.

She swayed, staggered forward, but the room spun in a circle, the white whirling around and around. Stars exploded in front of her eyes, pinpoints of light flickering like fireflies. Matilda pushed her back onto the bed. She tried to fight, but her limbs were so heavy she couldn't make them cooperate. Luke's face flashed into her mind just before she succumbed to the exhaustion and curled onto her side.

She felt the brush of the comforter whisk over her legs as Matilda covered her, then heard the door close and the lock shift into place.

Seconds later, she was alone again. Just like she had been years ago.

Just as she would always be.

No one knew where she was. No one was coming back for her. No one loved Stella.

And no one could save her...

AFTER THREE DAYS, Devlin had had enough stalling from Sutton. The photos had definitely raised his doubts. And he had discovered that Sutton had contributed financially to CIRP, cementing a connection. The conversation with the reporter haunted him. Stella had used him. Had been working against him.

Was it possible?

He cursed and grabbed his keys, but his cell phone rang, and he checked the ID.

Myra, J.T.'s wife. "Hello."

"Luke, hey…I just wanted to check in."

"How're you doing?"

"Okay."

She sounded depressed again. "What's wrong, Myra? Missing J.T.?"

"It's not me, it's little Jimmy. He dreamed about him last night."

"That's rough." Luke sighed, tired, feeling as if he'd let her down as he had J.T. and Stella. "I'll drop by there soon, take him out for the day."

"Thanks, Luke. I'd appreciate it. Any news on the investigation?"

Guilt struck Luke for putting J.T.'s case on hold for his own selfish purposes. "No."

"What about your wife?"

He hesitated, then told her everything except that he suspected the two cases might be related. He just didn't know how yet. J.T. had worked undercover to find out what kinds of top secret research CIRP might be conducting. J.T. had discovered cloning experiments. And Luke had met Stella shortly after J.T.'s death… The timing seemed too coincidental.

"Gosh, Luke, I'm sorry. And here I am whining to you."

"It's okay, that's what friends are for. Listen, Myra,

I put a check in the mail today. You should have it in a couple of days."

"You don't have to keep sending money, Luke."

"It's for J.T." And you and little Jimmy, he wanted to say. The family he'd never had.

But he refrained. He didn't want to give Myra the wrong idea. He'd never see her as anything but J.T.'s wife.

"I'll keep you posted if I turn up anything. Take care."

He hung up and glanced outside at the clouds rolling in.

It was nearly night once again, and Sutton hadn't returned any of his calls. Luke headed to his car, climbed in and pulled into the late-evening traffic.

He was finished being told that Stella was resting. That she couldn't be disturbed. That the doctors had ordered complete bedrest.

Sutton was up to something, and Luke intended to pay him a surprise visit and find out exactly what he was hiding.

It was almost as if Sutton had sequestered Stella away from everyone else, so he could manipulate her or the situation. But why? Because the reporter was right, and Sutton was involved in Stella's espionage activities.

He muttered a curse. He had no concrete proof that the reporter's information was correct.

The pictures certainly hadn't been conclusive. And when Luke had phoned in a few favors at the bureau, no one had known anything about such an operation.

The feds had been looking for Stella for over a year

now. If someone had suspected her of spying, wouldn't they have told him?

Not if they thought you were involved.

Although in light of this new possibility, Spencer Grossman's suspicious reactions to Luke the last year took on a new meaning. The man was looking for a reason to fire Luke. Had even suggested that Luke might have been involved in J.T.'s death.

A light switch flicked on in his head. If Grossman thought Stella had converted Luke to her side, then they would have treated him as the enemy. Kept him out of the loop. Uninformed.

His mind ticked away the pieces of the puzzle. The mysterious events and experiments at Nighthawk Island flashed back, giving the entire situation a sinister feeling.

Except so far, barring the location of Sutton's estate and his donations, Luke had found no connection between Sutton and the research facility. And the police hadn't yet determined the identity of the man who'd been murdered in Stella's motel room.

What was Luke missing?

And why didn't Sutton want Stella to see him? Was he afraid she'd remember something? Admit to him that she was a spy? That she'd used him all along?

Bitterness and hurt swelled inside of him, robbing him of air as he drove toward Sutton's residence. He would see Stella tonight or use his trump card and threaten to arrest Sutton and take Stella into custody himself.

Then he'd make her talk.

He approached the iron gates with determination,

rolled down the window, the heat suffusing him as he pressed the security buzzer, then waited for security to reply. "Special Agent Luke Devlin here to see Mr. Sutton and Stella Segall."

"Do you have an appointment, sir?"

"No, but tell Sutton if he doesn't let me in this time, I'm calling backup with a warrant and slapping him with a bail violation hearing. And if I do that, I'll make sure Stella Segall is removed from his estate."

A long, tense silence vibrated in the air as he waited on the reply. Seconds later, the sound of the buzzer announced he'd succeeded in making his point. He gripped the steering wheel with sweaty fingers as he tackled the driveway, his gaze scanning the property. High-tech cameras dotted the wooded area, indicating that Sutton probably maintained a state-of-the-art security system.

For protection, or to keep people out of his private compound? And who exactly did Sutton need protection from?

It damn sure couldn't be to protect his prized paintings.

Then again, Luke had never been into art.

Except in the form of a beautifully shaped woman like Stella.

He consciously banished that thought with a reminder that Stella might be a spy and had probably cozied up to him hoping to extract secret, confidential information about Nighthawk Island from him.

If so, why had she left though?

Unless she'd been found out by an enemy…

If so, who? One of his colleagues? Someone who'd withheld the information from him because they suspected he was a traitor too?

STELLA HAD FINALLY awakened before dinner and dragged herself into the shower. She was determined to stay awake and speak to Sutton. And if he refused, she'd discover a way out of this place and track down Luke Devlin.

She rang the intercom, asked for Sutton and was surprised when he showed up five minutes later.

"How are you feeling this evening, dear?" he asked as he entered her sitting room.

She twisted her fingers together. "Better, Mr. Sutton."

"Oh, honey, please call me Drake. You always have."

She nodded, although she still felt uncomfortable in his presence. "All right, Drake, I've asked Matilda to stop giving me those injections. They make me so groggy I can't function."

"You needed rest, Stella," Drake said. "Doctor's orders."

"But the drugs triggered nightmares."

"What kind of nightmares?"

Stella hesitated weighing her choices. If Sutton was going to help her, she had to admit the truth. "About being a killer."

Sutton nodded. "From the other night?"

"Yes," she said in a low voice. She studied her hands for a minute, remembered the blood on her fingers.

"What else do you remember, Stella?"

She met his gaze, saw understanding in his eyes. Acceptance.

"I dreamed that someone told me to kill Luke Devlin. Then I took a .38 and shot him."

A slow smile spread across his lips. "Obviously that hasn't happened."

"No." But it still disturbed her. "Have I ever done anything like this before?"

"You're referring to your memory loss or the shooting?"

Stella swallowed hard, not certain if she wanted the answer. "Both."

He crossed one suited leg over the other, then glanced away as if biding his time. "Yes."

Stella clutched her hands together as that revelation sank in.

"I'm not sure you're ready to hear about your background yet."

"Hear what? What's wrong with me? Am I mentally ill?" That might explain her panicked reaction to the hospital.

"No, Stella, you're not mentally ill. You're a very intelligent, ingenious young woman."

"Then tell me the truth. My body has had enough rest—I can take it. But I can't keep going on in this blind tunnel not knowing who I am or what kind of person I was. Or if I'm going to prison for murder."

Drake's dark brows furrowed. "I promised you I'd take care of the situation, and I will. I should hear from your attorney tomorrow."

Her gaze shot to his. "Have I talked to Luke Devlin?"

Drake frowned. "Actually he's here now. The butler is supposed to show him to my study. I'm meeting him in just a moment."

Stella heaved a relieved breath. Maybe she'd been

overreacting, imagining that Drake Sutton was holding her prisoner.

"Can I go with you? I'd like to hear what he has to say."

He hesitated, then narrowed his eyes. "Only if you listen to me first." He crossed the room, glanced out the window, then pivoted back toward her with a grim but resigned expression. "You're right. You need to know what's going on, so you can monitor your conversation when you talk to Devlin."

"I don't understand."

Evening shadows played along his jaw, adding to his intimidating stance. "Stella, you are part of a secret organization of spies. Agent Devlin was investigating Nighthawk Island, and was about to expose us. Your last assignment was to cozy up to Agent Devlin, seduce him if necessary, then kill him to protect us."

Stella gasped and rocked back in shock. The nightmare she'd had this morning was supposed to have really happened? She was a hired killer?

She stared at her hands in renewed horror. Of all the scenarios she'd feared hearing, that hadn't been one of them.

She grappled to make her voice work. "What about the man in the motel room?"

Drake shrugged. "That man, Raul Jarad, was your handler. Someone got to him, though, turned him. He was going to give you up." Drake made a clicking sound with his teeth. "A shame, but Jarad had to be taken care of."

Disbelief roared through Stella's head. His story was too horrible to be true. Drake was lying. She couldn't kill someone in cold blood. And she wasn't a spy...

Flashes of the erotic dreams of Luke raced back. Luke naked and taking her to bed. Stripping her clothes slowly and teasing her legs apart. Whispering to her in the dark. Loving her until morning. Touching every inch of her naked body. Torturing her until she could do nothing but breathe his name, feel his lips on her skin and memorize the taste of him forever.

Had their romance been a lie? An act on her part?

Her gaze rose to meet Sutton's, the atmosphere charged with tension. "Does Luke Devlin know that I'm a s-spy?" There she'd said it, but she still didn't believe it.

Drake's mouth flattened into a thin line. "It's possible. That's one reason you need to be wary, Stella. You were playing up to him to kill him, essentially sleeping with the enemy." He hesitated. "I'm not sure what his motive was. He might have figured out your motive, and he went along to lure you into a false sense of security before he took you down."

Realization dawned like a knife stabbing Stella. If Drake wasn't lying, and Luke had known her identity, then he had probably planned to arrest her all along. Maybe she'd figured out that he was onto her, and that was the reason she'd disappeared on their wedding night.

In any case, it meant that Luke didn't really care for her. That he'd made love to her and married her for his own deceptive reasons. And that once again, there was no one she could trust.

Chapter Six

Luke studied the sleek cherrywood desk and leather furnishings in Drake Sutton's study. Not only had the foyer been filled with expensive, original artwork, but his office showcased similar pricey pieces. That and several crystal flutes filled with pricey liquor, Waterford wine goblets, highball glasses, champagne flutes, and ashtrays that cost more than Luke's own cabin on Skidaway Island. An elaborate computer system completed the office, one which would also put Luke's to shame. He wondered what type of security Sutton had on the machine. What kind of secret businesses he indulged in.

More importantly, he desperately wanted to know what Sutton was doing with Stella.

Had he hurt her? Touched her...?

Stella. God, he had to put that spark of emotion that reared to life at the thought of her in its place. He had important decisions to make—like how to play it with Stella. If she'd truly lost her memory, she wouldn't be able to explain her actions in the pictures the reporter had shown him. That fact gave him the advantage.

An advantage he fully intended to use.

Just as she had used him.

He searched his memory for a reason why she might have targeted him specifically. The only case high on his priority at the moment, other than hers, was the research facility at Nighthawk Island. In fact, when they'd met, he'd been coordinating with a team of medically trained agents in D.C. to choose an agent to go undercover at the facility. He'd decided on Quinn Salt, a special ops forces agent who had majored in bioengineering and medical sciences, and had worked in various areas of biological and chemical warfare research for the government. Luke's partner, J.T., had been undercover for a while.

Then he'd ended up dead.

Was that the reason Stella had come onto him? Did she want or have information about the secret projects being conducted on Nighthawk Island? Then why not go straight to the scientists? Or maybe she wanted to find out how much he knew? She could have fed him false information to protect Sutton's secrets But they had *never* discussed the research part. They'd been too busy...

Irritation needled him at the mere idea that he'd been such a sucker. He strode to the window and peered through the glass at the wooded area that encompassed Sutton's property.

What had happened to his suspicious nature where Stella was involved? He'd never let down his guard before, never allowed a woman or any other suspect to snowball him in such a way.

Never let sex detract him.

Hell, he'd had lots of women before Stella. So many

that their faces blurred into a virtual sea of strangers lost in his own memory. Just as the evenings he'd spent with them had.

All meaningless sexual encounters that had sated him physically but left him emotionally barren.

Which was the way he'd preferred it. Uncomplicated.

Until Stella...

But her touch had made him delirious. Made him lose his sanity. Dream about a future. Get married.

God, he'd been such a fool.

"You're a gutless failure." His father's words echoed in his head over and over. The constant put-downs. The expectations. The battles over what Luke would do with his life. His father had wanted him to join him in the business. A theft ring that had been famous for stealing jewelry from trusting women.

Law enforcement was the last thing his father would have chosen for him.

Maybe that explained why Luke had gravitated toward it.

The streets had needed cleaning of scumbags like his old man, and he'd taken it upon himself to do just that. Still, he hadn't had the courage to actually lock up his father. But he'd never crossed the line to protect him, either.

God help him if his dad ever got out of jail. Over the years, Luke had worked up nerves of steel. And his conscience had been destroyed.

Sure, he'd taken advantage of women. He'd used them in undercover assignments without batting an eye, which technically put him on par with his father—

something he wasn't proud of. But he had always done whatever necessary to complete the job, because ultimately enforcing the law meant protecting the innocent.

He fisted his hands and stared at the elaborate pattern of the oriental rug on the hardwood floor.

Yes, he'd always done what he needed to do to get results. Even if it meant hurting people.

His father would laugh his ass off at the irony. Even though Luke had fought it, had turned to law instead of a life of crime, the liar gene must have been in his bloodstream. In some ways he'd turned into his old man. Ruthless. Calculating. Detached.

Yet he'd screwed up a year ago. And all for a pretty woman.

"Mr. Devlin?"

Luke froze, schooling his reaction as he pivoted and faced Sutton. "You finally agreed to see me. I was losing my patience."

"Ahh, a federal agent who isn't a patient man," Sutton said smoothly. "Why doesn't that surprise me?"

"I told you I'd be back. You can't ignore the FBI, Sutton."

"I had no intention of doing such a thing, but I've been otherwise entertained."

He hoped to hell not with Stella.

Get a grip. He was probably talking business. Attorneys. Luke would ask about that later. "Where's Stella?"

A small smile quirked Sutton's mouth. "She's right here. I forewarned her that you'd probably want to speak with her."

Luke narrowed his eyes. He'd expected Sutton to refuse. Had been prepared to pull out all the punches. Had half hoped he would so that Luke could throw his weight around and remove her from the premises.

"Is she all right?"

"She was exhausted, but my staff has taken excellent care of her. Physically she's recovering, but her memory still hasn't returned."

"I want to see her." Luke's chest tightened at the words. If only he didn't want it so much.

"She's waiting outside." Sutton walked to the door, opened it and gestured with a wide sweep of his hand for her to enter.

Luke's jaw tightened as he struggled to maintain his composure and not touch her.

STELLA GRIPPED Drake Sutton's arm as she entered his study. She was still reeling from the information he'd given her upstairs, so much so that she wasn't prepared to face Luke Devlin.

If she were the awful person Sutton had described, and Luke knew the truth, there was no telling what he was thinking. Maybe he was here to haul her back to jail. Maybe he wanted revenge.

Maybe he wanted to kill her.

She shivered, her knees wobbling, and clutched at Sutton for support. In another instant, she wondered why. Drake had just proclaimed that *she* was a killer And he'd smiled as he'd announced it, as if he was proud. As if he had created her himself.

Drake patted her hand in silent comfort and led her to the brown leather sofa, then handed her a drink of water. She almost asked for a scotch, then paused to wonder if that was her favorite drink, or if she was simply feeling desperate.

One look into the mask that comprised Luke's expression, and she flinched. In that second, another emotion flickered in his black eyes—hunger. A tingle traveled down her center and into her belly. The titillating dream floated back, temporarily destroying images of murder, and she smiled, the exquisite memory of his hands on her body doing unspeakably sensual things to her, stirring her to arousal. She was already wet from wanting this man. Her nipples budding to hardened peaks. Her womanhood throbbing for him to fill her.

God, he must have been good.

Guilt and shame quickly shattered the euphoria. If she had seduced Luke with the intention of killing him, and he didn't know, that meant she had been successful. That she was the cold, calculating, deceptive person Drake had painted her to be.

And Luke had been a victim.

But looking at the sexy, mysterious man in front of her, she had a difficult time believing she could have ever fooled him.

And if she were the cunning killer Drake had described, maybe she'd forgotten her past for a reason. Maybe to escape it.

"Are you feeling better, Stella?" Luke's husky voice skated over raw nerve endings.

She nodded, trembling as if he *had* touched her. Maybe she had wanted to escape the past.

Maybe she'd married Luke Devlin because she had actually fallen for him.

"ARE YOU SURE?" Luke asked. "You're shaking."

"I'm fine." She clutched one of the pillows on the sofa into her lap as if she needed to hang on to something.

He almost whispered that she could hang on to him, then caught himself, once again wondering why the sight of Stella rattled him from his normal composure. He had a job to finish, and he damn well had to stay on track.

Even if it meant lying to his wife so he could slap her back in jail.

Or playing the worried husband to win her confidence.

"What exactly did you need to discuss with us?" Sutton asked.

Luke detected an edge in Sutton's tone and silently admitted he enjoyed putting the man on the defensive. "I wanted to see if Stella remembered anything about the murder."

Stella clamped her teeth down on her lip and looked up at him. "No. Nothing."

"Did you identify the dead man yet?" Sutton asked.

"We're still working on that," Luke said. "In fact, we suspect he might be involved with Nighthawk Island."

Sutton shifted, one knuckle rapping against the solid wooden desk. Luke smiled. He'd struck a nerve.

Which meant that his guess had been correct. Sutton and the dead man were connected. And both might lead back to Nighthawk Island.

He had to warn Quinn that someone might be onto them, and to be wary of any contacts with relation to Sutton. He didn't want Quinn to end up like J.T.

"What is Nighthawk Island?" Stella asked.

Luke angled his head toward her. "It's a private research facility affiliated with the Coastal Island Research Park, also known as CIRP. There are research and hospital facilities on Catcall Island as well as Whistlestop Island and Nighthawk Island."

"What kind of research?" Stella asked.

"A wide variety of medically related projects," Luke answered. "The scientists conduct experiments on everything from stem cell research to biological and chemical warfare to psychological experimentation and treatments. The latest cutting-edge techniques are housed in the facilities with leading scientists from around the world lecturing and collaborating on highly secretive government projects."

Stella's ebony eyebrows rose. "All of that is being done here in Savannah?"

Luke nodded. "That's right. There's been some controversy surrounding some of the projects, cloning for one. At least two scientists have been killed because of research being sold to foreign governments, one policeman was brainwashed with a memory transplant surgical procedure, and recently a strange virus that caused suicidal tendencies was connected to the park."

Stella frowned. "I don't understand what that has to do with me, or the man who was murdered in the motel room."

Luke shrugged. "We're not certain yet, either." He slanted his gaze toward Sutton. "But we'll unearth the truth sooner or later."

Sutton gave him a cold stare. "If that's it, you should go, Agent Devlin."

Luke shook his head. "I'd like a few moments alone with Stella."

Stella's face paled.

Sutton shook his head. "Not without her lawyer present."

Luke feigned innocence. "You're forgetting something, Sutton. Stella is my wife."

"And she remembers nothing about that mistake," Sutton snapped.

"I...don't mind speaking with him," Stella said, surprising him.

Sutton's arms stiffened by his side. "I can't let you do that, Stella."

Luke sat stone-cold still, waiting for Stella's reply. Hoping she'd insist.

It was obvious from the way she squashed the pillow in her hands that Sutton intimidated her. Was she afraid to speak in front of him?

But why? What kind of hold did the man have over her?

And if Sutton's game was intimidation, Luke would do the opposite—play the loving concerned husband. If she was a spy as that reporter claimed, pretending innocence would work to his advantage.

"I simply want to speak to her privately." Luke dove into the role, turned to Stella and lowered his voice. "If we discuss the time we spent together, it might jog your memory, Stella. Details might help you recall how we met, how we fell in love, what we meant to one another."

Stella's eyes softened, her lips parting as if she actually wanted that, too.

He braced himself against her reaction. Just because she didn't remember using him before didn't mean that she hadn't.

Or that she wouldn't again if her memory returned.

STELLA HAD BEEN mesmerized by the sound of Luke's voice. He morphed from a stone-cold professional to a charming man in ten seconds. She could almost believe he wanted her to recall their affair and marriage, that it had been real.

But could she trust him? Or was his charm only a ruse?

If Sutton had told her the truth, and Luke knew the woman behind Stella Segall's act, then he might be playing her now to get revenge. If not, then God help her…she wanted to turn back time.

Lead a different life.

Let their relationship be real and erase the past.

Sutton took her arm, and she walked him to the door of the study. He stopped abruptly, then lifted a hand to the base of her neck and massaged the tight knot. "Be careful, Stella," he murmured. "This man works for the FBI. You're still facing murder charges."

As if she could forget.

She swallowed hard and nodded. Sutton squeezed her neck again, this time a little harder, and she read it as a warning. Obviously Sutton had secrets to protect, and he feared she'd expose him.

She wouldn't. Not until she knew the truth about everything. After all, at the moment Sutton was the only person standing between her and prison. And she couldn't go back to that cell.

She'd die inside.

Drake closed the door behind her, and she turned back to see Luke studying her. A frisson of nerves assaulted her. She had no idea what to say. What to do.

"Come and sit back down, Stella," he murmured. "I'm not going to bite."

"Would you like something to drink?"

He shook his head. "No. I just want to talk to you."

She nodded reluctantly, then slowly walked back to the sofa and claimed the same seat she'd occupied earlier. Luke settled into the leather wing chair opposite her, scooting it closer, so near their knees brushed. She looked up into his eyes and tried to read him, but didn't have a clue as to the inner workings of his mind.

Unbidden, the memory of the kiss at the prison rushed back to taunt her, and she folded her hands in her lap, perspiration beading her neck.

"We met in D.C.," Luke began in a low voice. "I saw you at a bar. You were sipping a watermelon martini."

She smiled at his husky tone.

"You were wearing the sexiest dress I'd ever seen. It dipped low to show off your figure and hugged you all over. It was so tight I wanted to peel it off."

"What were you doing in D.C.?" she asked, desperate to tear herself from the sex appeal in his eyes.

"I was there on business," he replied. "I'd suffered through several long grueling days of meetings. Briefings. Some about Nighthawk Island."

She was surprised he'd offered her that information.

"It was the last night, and I needed to unwind, so I chose a piano bar and restaurant near the hotel. A blues singer had been playing, and you walked up to the piano and dropped a tip in the jar. I had to meet you."

She glanced up, searched for deception, but the desire flaring in his eyes was so hot it had to be real. So, maybe she had used him, or he'd used her. But the attraction, the sex had been immediate. Real. Hot. Hungry. Raw.

A tingle of pure liquid heat rippled through her. On some level, she realized that she'd never been with a man like Luke Devlin. Never been touched or loved in such an animalistic way. A way that had bound her to him, even if it had been against her will.

"I asked you to dance," he said with a twitch of a smile. "And you said yes."

How could she not have? He was completely irresistible...

"Your hair was blond then," he continued. "Short and spiked with all kinds of waves that spiraled around your face. It looked like cornsilk, and I couldn't resist running my fingers through it while we swayed to the music."

"I...I'm sorry I don't remember," she said, mesmerized.

"But I do, Stella." He hesitated, ran a shaky hand over his chest.

Her heart fluttered. Had she really affected this man on some kind of emotional level? Had it not all been lies and deception?

"You're a sexy man," she whispered. "You've probably had a lot of women."

He shrugged. "None that mattered."

The words hung in the air between them, charged. Daring her to protest.

But God help her, she liked the sound of those words. Had never heard them from a man.

Or had she?

No, she instinctively knew she hadn't. Especially if she was the despicable woman Drake had claimed her to be.

Shame, regret, fear mounted inside her. She didn't want to be that woman. She ached to be the one Luke described. A sexy, loving woman, not a killer.

"We had a couple of drinks," Luke said. "Then we rushed to my hotel room nearby. We were tearing off each other's clothes before we even got in the door."

The image flashed into Stella's mind. A memory. Short but erotic.

Luke spoke the truth about that night. She remembered. Clung to it.

She'd been happy in his arms.

Sutton's words rushed back to taint the memory, though. Had she only been acting a part?

Luke reached out and traced a finger down her cheek. "Your skin felt like satin," he whispered roughly. "And your lips tasted like…like sweet watermelon. Innocent but decadent. And your hands… I've never had anyone else's fingers turn my body into a mass of need before. Not like yours."

Stella's entire body tingled. He twisted a strand of her hair around his finger, wound it around his thumb, drawing her face closer.

"I teased your lips apart like this." His other hand rose to tip up her chin, and his lips brushed hers. Tender. Hungry. Asking for more. His tongue played along the seam of her lips until she opened to him. He thrust himself inside, exploring, feeling, eliciting more desire. Deeper. Deeper. Deeper.

Her insides screamed for release. For her to be naked beside him. On top of him. Below him. Any way he'd take her.

He traced one finger along her collarbone, then down to her breasts, and his hand closed over her. Stroking. Teasing. Bringing her nipple to an aching peak of desire.

His mouth left hers, his breath a whisper against her cheek. "Then I dipped my head and tasted you here." His fingers pinched her nipple, and she moaned.

"We made love for hours, Stella. And not just that night. But every night after." He kissed her again, this time more forceful, thrusting his tongue so far in her mouth she gripped his arms for support. He moved to the sofa, took her in his lap, and pushed her skirt up her thighs. Not asking. Taking.

Cool air brushed her bare skin, but the rest of her went ablaze with fire as he slowly trailed his fingers along the insides of her thighs. With a small moan, he mimicked the motion of sex as his body moved against hers. She bucked and moaned, craving the touch of his bare skin. His shirt buttons gave way easily, and her hands found their way inside. Touching. Feeling. Rasping over his coarse chest hair, tingling as his muscles bunched in her palms.

He groaned and suckled her neck, biting at her earlobe, then dipped his head to tease her nipples beneath the shirt. Seconds later, his fingers slipped inside her panties, eased away the lacy barrier until they slid inside her. She gulped in air, felt heat scald her face. She should pull away. Stop this insanity.

But he was like a drug. Addictive. Hypnotizing her with his titillating touch.

He tightened his embrace, and kissed her again, this time hard, fast, urgent as his fingers dipped deeper inside her, thrusting first one, then two, then three through the dampness until she felt herself coming apart. He pushed deeper, slid his fingers out to play with her feminine lips, to taunt her rosebud of desire, to bring her to flames. Colors flashed before her eyes as waves of satisfaction rippled through her.

She moaned his name in a throaty whisper as she hung onto his arms and savored the ride.

LUKE WAS ON the verge of forgetting himself and his job, of freeing his aching erection and sating his hunger, but someone knocked at the door. Stella panted, clinging to his neck, her hair falling across his cheek as she leaned into him.

"Stella?" His voice rumbled out a husky croak, thick with pent up passion.

The knock sounded again, finally penetrating the air between them with an awkwardness steeped in tension. Stella still quivered from her orgasm. And he still craved his own.

Neither one of them wanted company.

"Agent Devlin."

Sutton's commanding voice boomed through the closed doorway, and he heaved a breath. "Just a minute."

Stella lifted her head and looked into his eyes, her dark hair spilling around cheeks rosy from their lovemaking. The passion lingering in her sultry gaze nearly brought him to his knees. But confusion flickered also, triggering a momentary sense of guilt.

She had remembered their lovemaking, at least to a point—he felt it in her response. But too many unanswered questions stood between them, a broken trust that tainted the flavor of their ecstasy.

He righted her skirt, and she slid off his lap, thumbing her slender fingers through her tangled hair while he rebuttoned his shirt. What the hell had he been thinking? That he could seduce her into remembering everything? Into admitting that she was a spy, that she'd used him? That she'd never loved him?

Or that he was such a potent lover, that she had fallen for him as well? That she never could have deceived him, never could have destroyed their special bond...

Yet she had destroyed it the minute she'd left him on their wedding night.

Stella squared her shoulders and walked toward the door, her hips swaying seductively. He envisioned that slinky thong below the skirt and wanted her again, this time his sex thrusting inside her all the way. The scent of her lingered on his hands, her moans of pleasure echoing in his ears.

She opened the door and Sutton walked in, frowning. Above the doorway, Luke noticed small surveillance cameras tucked into the corners of the room. They were built-in, hidden, so that the untrained eye wouldn't detect them.

But he was a professional.

He should have checked for them earlier. Should have realized that the entire compound was probably wired and rigged so that Sutton could protect his possessions. His secrets.

Sutton considered Stella one of those possessions.

And judging from his icy expression, he'd been watching while Luke had ripped Stella's skirt up her thighs and nearly rammed himself inside her.

Chapter Seven

Stella was still rocking inside from her climax, still pondering how amazing it had felt to have Luke's fingers deeply embedded inside her, when Drake Sutton walked in. But his presence, along with the stony expression on his face, made any lingering euphoria vanish quickly. Shame and embarrassment replaced it.

"I think you've taken enough of our time for today," Drake announced. "So, unless you're here to drop the charges against Stella, then you should go, Agent Devlin."

Stella sucked in a sharp breath as Luke stood. His calm demeanor seemed at odds with his rigid stance. It was almost as if he were exerting extraordinary control on his baser impulses, preparing for a standoff between himself and her host.

"I can't have the charges dropped." Luke's cold tone matched Drake's. "Not without more evidence. Do you have information you'd like to share with me, Sutton? Like the identity of the man in Stella's hotel room? Or the reason they were together?"

Sutton shrugged. "I refuse to answer any questions without my attorney present."

"Your secrecy in itself makes you look suspicious." Luke stepped closer to Drake. "If you'd cooperate and answer our questions, we could clear up this matter more quickly. I want to know where Stella was the past thirteen months. Why she really ran out on our wedding night. The real reason you never came forward to say that you knew her when the news flashed her picture after she disappeared."

"I told you I travel internationally. I was out of the country most of last year, and I also know she wanted to be free of you." Drake inhaled sharply. "Now if you'd do your job and find the real person responsible for that man's death the other night, it would expedite matters for Stella."

"I am doing my job," Luke replied. "Helping Stella regain her memory is one of the key elements in solving this crime."

"Is that what you were doing?" Drake asked.

Stella's face heated. Did Drake know what had happened between her and Luke? If so, how?

A sick feeling washed over her as possibilities floated through her mind. Drake had claimed he ran a secret organization. The entire house was surrounded with security. What if he had cameras in the rooms?

Her gaze shot around the study searching. To the bookcase filled with original collections. The mantel clock. The corners, the vents.

But she didn't see anything that resembled a camera.

"Stella," Luke said, jarring her from her thoughts. "I will go now. But only if you leave with me."

Drake gave her a warning look. She couldn't. She

had more questions about her past, and Drake was the one to answer them. "I can't," she said softly.

Luke hesitated a moment longer, and she almost relented. But the power Luke possessed was as potent as Sutton's. Except Luke's hold was more sexual. More dangerous.

Luke cleared his throat. "If you need anything, please call me. And if you remember any details about that night, let me know." He squeezed her hand, his dark gaze meeting hers for a fraction of a second. In it, she saw concern, distrust, the remnants of sexual desire.

And disappointment that she'd chosen Sutton over him.

Confusion almost swayed her to change her mind and vault toward Luke. But the dream about her mother taunted her.

Still, if Drake were telling the truth and she'd wanted free of Luke, why had she responded so quickly to his lovemaking?

Luke stalked from the room leaving her alone with Drake Sutton and her growing suspicions that he was not the friend he claimed to be.

"Wipe that dazed look off of your face, Stella," Drake barked. "Luke Devlin is a first-class agent. He's using you, and you're falling into his trap. Again."

The air tightened in her throat. "What do you mean *again?*"

"You seduced him before, but he seduced you as well." He made a disgusted sound. "It's obvious he still has that power over you."

"What do you mean by that?"

"You damn well nearly screwed him on the couch!"

His shout startled her. But his words confirmed her earlier suspicions. "You have cameras in here? You've been watching me ever since you brought me home."

He chuckled. "Of course. They're everywhere, Stella. For your protection as well as mine." He paced across the room, running his hand through his hair. "For God's sake, you've not only put yourself in jeopardy, but you've jeopardized our entire operation here. We have other agents to consider, the missions we have pending and underway. And now you've brought the FBI into my private compound. I'll eventually have to relocate everything." He turned back to face her, his eyes blazing with fury. "But I'm still trying to help you, Stella. To prevent you from going to jail because I care about you. At one time, you were one of my best. You can seduce men into anything. You're skilled, logical, and you've never let emotions interfere."

Not until Luke Devlin. The bitter undertones of his accusations stood between them like a brick wall.

But the sense of being watched, her privacy violated, made bile rise to her throat. How had she lived like this before? Being constantly monitored, using men for sex, killing…

Or hadn't she minded? Had she really been the seductive woman Drake claimed, the one who'd used people, even murdered, with emotional detachment?

Even if she had, she didn't want to return to that world. But how could she escape? Drake Sutton seemed to think he owned her. And she sensed an underlying danger to her core. That he didn't give up easily. Or allow his agents to leave him.

What would he do if she tried to escape?

Would Luke help her if she came clean?

Reality intervened. She was out on bail, pending a murder trial. All the evidence so far pointed to her. And he was one of the investigating agents. He'd have to put her back in jail.

No, she couldn't go back to prison.

The memory of Luke's touch drifted back, and her body tingled anew with desire. He'd felt it, too. Hadn't he?

Or was Drake right—was Luke using her? Or had the passion between them been real?

LUKE'S CELL PHONE rang as soon as he settled in his car. He flipped it open. "Special Agent Devlin."

"Devlin, this is Marvin Andrews from the *Sun*."

"What do you want?" Luke snapped.

"I have a disk I'm sending to your house. Just look at it, then call me."

Without another word, the phone clicked into silence.

Luke cursed, frustrated with the reporter, with the case, with his own damn self.

He cut into the streets, blinking at the blinding car lights and drove into downtown Savannah toward the police station to confer with the local Savannah cops. Maybe they'd learned something about the man Stella had allegedly murdered. He sure as hell hadn't made any headway.

The town was alive with action, tourists roaming the sidewalks, happy-hour partiers overflowing the bars where blues and jazz music floated through the streets, the hub of River Street welcoming to the young and old alike. He envisioned the happy couples strolling along the waterfront the way he'd imagined when Stella and he had first married over a year ago, but their life had been clouded by her disappearance. His marriage was, he now suspected, a complete sham. It had been from the beginning.

Although neither he nor Stella had acted as if that were true a few minutes earlier.

He reminded himself he had been seducing Stella into remembering him, their past, that he needed to win her trust so she would confide in him, and he could find out exactly who she was. If she had intentionally hooked up with him to finagle information from him.

But she had seduced him in the process. Those throaty little moans. The way her lips had parted, nearly begging him inside. The way her hips had twitched, and her legs had opened for him, squeezing and gripping his fingers, her body clenching against his skin with her orgasm.

He imagined Sutton watching and a mixture of emotions speared him. Contempt that he hadn't noticed the camera earlier. Suspicions that Sutton had put Stella up to coming onto him. Distrust of the man's so-called international businesses. They had to be a front for something else. But what? Drug running? Money laundering?

And why hadn't he interrupted earlier? Had he hoped Stella would seduce information out of Luke?

Sutton's face flashed back, as well as the realization that Sutton disliked seeing Luke and Stella together. The man didn't exercise as much control over Stella as Luke had first thought, or feared. Stella had given something to *him* that she'd never shared with Sutton.

"You're a damn fool," he muttered. Stella might have been faking her reaction all along, using him.

Only she hadn't faked that orgasm.

Would he have played things differently if he'd known about the cameras?

Probably. He'd definitely have angled Stella's body away from Sutton so he wouldn't have glimpsed her bare thighs.

But he wasn't sure he would have stopped himself from taking all she had offered.

Hell, he wasn't sure he *could* have stopped—one kiss had set him on fire and robbed him of his senses.

But he was glad Sutton had witnessed Luke's power over Stella as well.

Did he have the power to completely take her away from the man?

Hell, who was he kidding? Stella hadn't been a virgin when they'd met. No telling how many men she'd seduced, slept with…

He reached the police station, veered into the parking lot, and climbed out, wiping sweat from his brow as the sultry temperatures engulfed him.

The hum of cops' voices surrounded him as he entered the station. He showed his ID to the desk sergeant, then quickly noted the activity. Two cops chowed down on Chinese food at their desks, a female officer was questioning a young woman in tears, and another teenager with sagging jeans and an arm full of tattoos sat sullen and handcuffed to a metal chair, bellowing about police brutality.

"All in a day's work," a chubby black officer muttered with a grin.

Luke nodded. Actually it seemed fairly calm. Must not be a full moon tonight.

Or maybe the real street action hadn't begun yet.

"Devlin."

He glanced up and saw Detective Black waving him to his office. Luke strode toward him, shook his hand, then stepped inside. Detective Fox sat scrutinizing a computer screen.

"Do we have anything on the dead man?" Luke asked.

Fox cut Black a look that spiked Luke's curiosity. "What?"

"You'd better sit down." Black gestured toward a wooden chair in the corner.

Luke shook his head. "I'll stand. Just tell me what you've got."

Fox and Black exchanged another awkward look. As if in silent agreement, Fox positioned the computer monitor so Luke could see it.

"We think we have a name on the vic," Fox said. "Raul Jarad."

"The name doesn't ring a bell. He has priors?"

"No. But we've had surveillance on Nighthawk Island for some time," Detective Black said, "and he's been spotted there on several occasions."

"In relation to what?" Luke asked.

"We're not sure yet. Your guy, Quinn Salt, is supposed to check him out for us."

Luke nodded. "So, he might know something about the medical experiments being conducted under the cuff?"

"Maybe." Fox shrugged. "But there's more."

"His name was also flagged in the bureau's database," Black reported.

"You received clearance to check there?" Luke asked.

"From Grossman, your superior, himself."

Luke frowned. "He didn't contact me."

Another awkward pause and Luke had his answer. Grossman didn't trust Luke, so he was withholding information.

"Look, detectives, spill it all. I'm being up front with you here. I just want the truth."

Black seemed to weigh his words, then nodded. "We think he's involved in espionage, that he was trying to steal medical research from Nighthawk Island. Chemical research for bio-terrorism is a big concern.

"We also think that he was trying to secure a contact within the bureau."

The implications echoed in the air between them as if they'd been voiced aloud.

"Through me?" Luke asked.

"That would be my guess," Fox said.

"And he intended to do that through my wife?"

"It seems feasible," Fox said.

"You didn't catch on?" Black asked.

Luke wanted to claim that he hadn't been an idiot, a fool who'd fallen for a woman, that he hadn't been seduced by her eyes and deceived by her beauty.

But if he lied now, he'd never win these men's trust. His reputation was on the line—it was more important than his pride.

"Not at first," Luke admitted sourly. "But a reporter contacted me a couple of days ago. He had pictures that indicated Stella might have been involved in espionage."

"When were you going to tell us this?" Black asked.

"I wanted to wait until I had more. This guy's some sleazeball for the *Sun.* I had no idea if his information was correct or if he was fishing for a story. And he didn't have any details about her assignments."

"You can't exactly ask Stella, can you?" Fox commented.

"That's right." No, instead he'd kissed her again, tried to tear off her clothes. God, he was losing it. And all over a lying woman.

"What else do you have on Jarad?"

"That's all for now. We're still looking," Fox said.

"Do you have a copy of those photos?" Black asked.

"No. But the reporter called me a few minutes ago, said he's sending me a disk with some information on it. If the lead pans out, I'll call you."

"Let's just hope he's not playing with us and wasting our time," Fox said.

Luke nodded. If he was, he'd make the scumball pay.

And if he had information that revealed someone had hurt Stella, he'd get revenge.

But if the information proved Stella was a traitor, it wouldn't matter how much Luke still wanted her. He'd have to go after her and see that she paid as well.

"COME WITH ME, Stella."

Stella twisted her hands together, anxiety plucking at her as she followed Drake.

After their conversation, he'd gone to the bar in the corner, poured a highball glass of scotch and offered it to her. When she'd declined, he'd downed it, then a second one without speaking.

"Where are we going?"

"You need to see something." He removed a book from the shelf of collectible, leather-bound volumes, and pressed a button, triggering the bookshelf to spin around, offering them entrance to what appeared to be a hallway.

Stella swallowed, her agitation rising. She suddenly didn't feel at all comfortable with Sutton. An image of another basement room rose from the grave to haunt her. A room where bad things happened. Pain. Sorrow. Torture. "What's down there?"

"Another set of offices." As if he realized her trepidation, he added, "Don't worry. I have an elaborate technological system downstairs that monitors all our operations. And two of our other agents are waiting to talk to you."

She narrowed her eyes, then followed him, the darkness swallowing her as they headed toward a distant light. A door separated the hall from the area, and Sutton removed a key card, swiped it through the security chamber, and the heavy wooden door slid open.

There, they faced an elevator which carried them to a large ground-floor room that was well lit, and filled with high-tech cameras, computers, tracking devices, and other sophisticated equipment.

Two women were stationed in front of the elaborate wall of computers, monitoring transmissions and entering data. He introduced them as Katrina Dixon, better known as Kat, and Jaycee Short.

The two women gave Stella an assessing, almost disapproving, look at the same time. Kat was tall, sleek, with dark, exotic eyes and angled features. Jaycee wore her auburn hair in a pixie cut, and her amber eyes matched her athletic warm-up suit.

But their icy expressions caused Stella to draw back.

"You don't remember them, do you?" Drake asked.

"No." In fact, she could have sworn she'd never met them.

"Do you have her under control?" the woman named Kat asked.

"We're working on reprogramming," Drake countered.

Stella stiffened at his choice of words.

Jaycee frowned, folding her arms across her chest. "We can't afford all this attention. I can't believe she led the feds here."

"I realize we're facing a conundrum," Drake said in an impatient tone. "But we'll meet the challenge."

"Are you sure she hasn't already leaked information about us to Devlin?" Jaycee asked.

Stella detested being talked about as if she weren't present. "How could I when I don't remember anything?"

"I mean before," Jaycee clarified. "When you were sharing pillow talk."

Drake threw up a warning hand. "We went over this thirteen months ago. At that time, we had no reason to think Stella betrayed us."

"If she did, the feds would already have found us," Kat added.

Drake nodded in agreement and Jaycee seemed to calm. "I want you to show Stella photos of past assignments," Drake said. "Jog her memory."

Kat nodded and punched in some keys on the elaborate keyboard in front of her.

"Once you see these, you'll believe me," Drake said. "Then we can discuss your next assignment."

"My next assignment?" Stella asked.

"Yes. You complete it, then we'll get these charges dropped, and I'll help acclimate you back into your old lifestyle."

Back to being a traitor and a murderer.

"Have you taken care of the evidence?" Drake asked Katrina.

She nodded with a smile. "Done. The police don't even know the gun is missing."

Drake gave her an approving smile, then gestured for Stella to sit in front of the computer. "We have information that a reporter stumbled onto photos of you that could be damaging to us."

"What kind of photos?" Stella asked. "What are you…we…doing here in Savannah?"

"We're here to retrieve information from Nighthawk Island," Kat interjected.

"You mean to steal their research?" Stella asked.

"There's a lot of people who want information on their projects," Jaycee added. "Some important people who are willing to pay well."

The wheels turned in Stella's mind, filing the possibilities, drawing conclusions about the people she apparently had worked for. They were talking about selling to foreign governments and scientists. Being traitors. The truth dawned. So, Drake made financial profits at any cost.

"Anyway," Drake said, sounding impatient, "he supposedly has a disk which could be very damaging to your case. You must retrieve the disk before Devlin sees it."

"How am I supposed to do that?" Stella asked.

Jaycee cursed. "She's a lost cause."

"Sneak into his place and steal it," Kat said in a flat voice.

Sneak into Luke's place? "And if that doesn't work?"

"Eliminate him," Jaycee said. "We'll find a way to dispose of his body so no one knows."

Stella's stomach churned. The memory of her love-making with Luke floated back, haunting her. Could she really kill Luke, even if it was to protect herself?

Drake traced a finger down her arm, a smirk on his face. "Or you could do what comes natural to you, Stella. You had him halfway there this afternoon."

Once again, shame and humiliation clogged Stella's throat. But how could she argue? She'd practically screwed Luke in Drake Sutton's study, and all because of one wild, amorous kiss. But that kiss had been about passion, not seduction for deceptive purposes.

Hadn't it?

"She's not going to convince Devlin to join our side," Jaycee said. "I've studied his profile. He won't bend."

Stella silently agreed. Luke Devlin wasn't the kind of man to refute his beliefs for anyone. He had strong morals.

Something she'd obviously been lacking. "What's on the disk?" she finally asked.

Drake's eyes darkened. "Proof that you're connected to the man you shot in the motel."

Stella's chest tightened. "So I did shoot him?"

"Yes." Drake made a sound with his cheek. "It had to be done. Unfortunately you blacked out and didn't get rid of the body."

"Why did I kill him?" Stella asked.

"He was on the verge of exposing our organization." Sutton's words sank in fast, making a chill run down her spine.

It was suddenly very clear that if anyone chose to betray Drake Sutton, whether they were on the outside or inside of his operations, the same thing would happen to them.

LUKE WAS ALMOST HOME when his cell phone jangled again. He dug into his pocket and retrieved it while he maneuvered the turn onto Skidaway Island where he'd rented a bungalow. "Special Agent Devlin."

"Detective Black. We just received the tox report on Stella Segall from the night of the murder."

Luke sucked in a breath. "And?"

"There are traces of sleeping pills in her system."

Which meant she might have been drugged. Other possibilities surfaced. Maybe she hadn't been alone with Raul Jarad. She could have blacked out and someone else could have killed Raul Jarad, framing her for the murder. "What about the autopsy on the victim?"

"The M.E. should have the report in the morning." Black hesitated. "We have another problem."

"I'm listening."

"The weapon that was used in the murder—it's missing."

Luke's hand tightened around the steering wheel. "What do you mean *missing?*"

"We followed the chain of custody to the T, but Detective Fox called CSI, and they relayed that it's not there."

Losing the gun would make trying Stella more difficult.

"Dammit," Luke muttered. "I have a hunch Sutton had something to do with this."

"My theory exactly," Black said. "We'll keep looking, but I thought I'd give you a heads-up. You may want to meet us at the M.E.'s office tomorrow morning."

Luke agreed and hung up, pulling a hand down his mouth. The gun was a key piece of circumstantial evidence. It would have probably cinched the case for the prosecution.

So why was a small part of him relieved to know it was missing?

Because it would give him time to work on Stella.

Stewing over the thought, he parked in front of the cabin, hopped out and strode up to the door. A sound inside jarred him, and he removed his gun, then silently inched around to the back door, crouching low as he checked the windows. A shadow flickered from his bedroom.

Someone was inside.

Instincts honed, he slowly let himself inside, treading softly so as not to alert the intruder of his presence. Seconds later, he moved to the doorway, poised his gun to fire, then slipped inside. The shadow darted to the closet, so he padded slowly toward the door, and tugged it open. The room and closet were dark, the swish of clothes filling the silence. Then a breath.

"FBI. Come out with your hands up."

His pulse accelerated as a woman slowly emerged. Stella.

She held a gun in her hand, her arm extended as if bracing for fire.

STELLA'S HAND shook so badly she could barely control it. Had she always been this nervous on an assignment?

"Stella, lower the gun," Luke ordered in a deep voice.

She bit down on her lip. There was no way out. If she didn't recover the disk, Drake Sutton would consider her a failure. And he might see her failure as a betrayal. Then her life would be worthless. If he'd stolen evidence, he could probably make it reappear and see that she was locked up for the rest of her life. Or he'd pump her with more drugs until she followed his commands.

Who was she kidding? Her life was worthless anyway. If she gave in to Luke, she'd be arrested again and sent to prison. But could she live knowing she'd killed him?

The air squeezed inside her lungs. The room swayed. Darkness engulfed her. Sweat beaded on her brow. She was losing it. She couldn't breathe. Couldn't move.

What was happening to her? "I can't go back to prison, Luke. It's too dark. Closed in. I can't see. I can't…breathe there."

Memories, nightmares bombarded her. Of being held prisoner. Being strapped down. Metal probes attached to her body. Shock waves jolting her.

A sob welled in her throat. She saw herself as a

child, struggling against the bindings. Being deprived of water. The ugly voices echoed in her head. Haunting her. Ordering her to obey. Reminding her that she had no choice.

A gun being shoved in her hand.

"Use it. Shoot now. You like to kill."

No! She didn't want to.

"Do it, Stella."

She tightened her finger on the trigger.

Luke cleared his throat. "Don't do it, Stella. You don't want to murder a federal officer, especially your husband."

She blinked, desperately struggling to banish the images from her mind. Luke's face shifted back into view. Those dark, enigmatic eyes. His steady gaze.

The memory of him touching her. Kissing her. Reassuring her that everything would be all right.

His fingers deep inside her.

She was so confused, her mind a wind tunnel of distant memories.

"You don't look well, Stella. Give me the gun and let's sit down."

His gaze remained even, his dark eyes piercing her with suspicions. But something else flared in his tone, a moment of sultry invitation that reminded her of their earlier encounter in the study.

Another brief memory flashed—the two of them making love. Whispering promises in the dark. The hope of freedom.

Had she used Luke, or had she really been in love with him? Maybe she'd viewed him as her ticket out of the life she used to lead. The one she didn't want to return to.

"I can't be locked up again, Luke. I won't survive...."

"Stella, I'm not taking you back to jail now. But you have to put down the gun and talk to me."

She shook her head. "You don't understand..." Her voice broke, hopes shattering just as her nerves crumbled. "I...I can't go back to Sutton's. It's a prison there, too. He drugged me."

Luke swallowed, the movement drawing her eye to the long column of his neck. To his shoulders. The ones she'd clung to this afternoon.

Her hand wavered. Fear raced through her. He reached out his hand for the gun.

Suddenly a shot sounded. Glass shattered. Luke lunged toward her and grabbed the weapon.

They crashed to the floor just as another bullet pinged through the air toward them.

Chapter Eight

Stella covered her head with her hands while Luke threw himself over her to protect her. Another bullet zinged near her shoulder, one hit a lamp and sent it crashing to the floor, and more glass exploded. Shards rained down on their heads and arms.

"We have to get out of here," Luke whispered. "Are you hit?"

"No." She lifted her head just enough to see his face. He was all right, too. Thank God. "Who's shooting at us?"

"I don't know," Luke hissed. "But follow me, and stay down."

Stella hunched down low and practically belly-crawled her way across the room to the small living area. Luke extended his arm for her to wait as he scanned the interior. "It's clear." More shots blasted through the bedroom window, then a bullet zinged through the sliding glass doors in front.

Déjà vu struck Stella, and she reacted on autopilot, skimming the room herself. Had Sutton or Kat and Jaycee followed her here? Maybe they hadn't trusted her to secure the disk or kill Luke.

And they were right. She couldn't have pulled the trigger.

"Come on," Luke said in a low voice.

He lurched to his feet, still crouching low, and dragged her up, then they raced through the room toward the door.

"I'll cover you, but stay down."

Stella nodded, but gripped her own weapon, ready to defend them as well.

He eased open the door, cut his gaze across the wooded area, then toward his sedan. "Now!"

Stella darted forward while he stepped onto the porch behind the wooden posts supporting the rails. She ran, zigzagging from side to side to dodge the bullets. As soon as she reached the car, she hurled open the door and threw herself inside.

Luke ran down the steps, firing, and she pressed the automatic window button, aimed her gun and shot a round to offer him cover. The realization that she'd done this before hit her as Luke circled the car.

Seconds later, Luke jumped inside, started the engine and tore down the driveway.

A bullet pinged off the bumper, another pelted the dash, and Luke yelled for her to get down. She ducked and fired back while he flew onto the main road away from the shooter.

"Damn it, that was an ambush. Who was it, Stella?"

She gaped at him, hating the accusations in his eyes. "I don't know."

"The hell you don't. You showed up searching for something, held a gun on me, then suddenly all hell breaks loose."

Stella glanced away from his damning eyes, contemplating how to reply. If she told him about Sutton's operation, she would be admitting to being a killer. To murdering the man in the motel. Then Luke would have to arrest her.

If she didn't —

"Jesus, Stella, you have to talk to me. Whoever shot at us back there wasn't just trying to kill me. They fired at you, too."

Stella stared at the scenery whirring past. Darkness engulfed her, the shadows of night resurrecting her nightmares.

Luke was right.

But who wanted her dead?

If she were the person Sutton had described, she might have dozens of enemies.

And if Sutton, Jaycee or Kat had followed her and sensed her hesitation over killing Luke, or thought she'd revealed their secrets, they would have no problem ending her life as well.

LUKE CHECKED the rearview mirror to see if they were being followed. So far, so good.

But he couldn't relax his guard. The entire situation reeked of a setup. Had his pretty bride been in on it? She'd known how to handle the gun, had been a natural. She obviously had experience.

So why was the shooter trying to kill her, too?

Unless they suspected she knew too much, or that she was close to spilling secrets.

Sutton.

It made perfect sense.

Stella clutched the seat edge with a white-knuckled grip, perspiration breaking out on her lower lip. He had to find out exactly what had happened at Sutton's.

And before that…he suspected there was more. A lot more to Stella's story. Things she didn't want to talk about or couldn't remember. Maybe she'd repressed her entire life for a reason.

Or maybe you're still looking for excuses to justify her actions.

Either way, the woman knew how to handle a gun. Had undergone training. Which made the reporter's theory more believable.

"What were you doing in my cabin?" he asked.

Stella inhaled sharply and thumbed her hair from her eyes. Blood dotted her palms, and shattered slivers of glass had settled into her skin. The fragments glinted in the dim light from the street light outside. She didn't seem to notice.

"I…came to talk to you."

A bold-faced lie. "Try again, Stella. If you'd wanted to talk, you wouldn't have pulled that gun."

"I…thought you were going to shoot me."

He narrowed his eyes. "You pulled the gun in self-defense?"

She nodded.

He shook his head again. "I'm still not buying it. Now, let's start over. Why did you come to my cabin?"

She twisted her fingers together as if struggling for a reply. Luke glanced up and noticed bright headlights race up on their tail.

"Dammit."

"What?"

"Someone's behind us. I'm calling for backup." He grabbed his phone and punched in Black's number.

Stella's eyes widened in fear as he sped up. The next few minutes, he maneuvered the car over the mile-long bridge toward Catcall Island, hoping to lose the shooters. Stella held onto the dashboard, the tension mounting as the car zoomed up on their rear. The driver gunned the engine and slammed into Luke's bumper. Luke swore and grappled for control. A shot pinged through the window. Stella ducked as he veered sideways. Back and forth, he swerved, dodging bullets. He darted over the drawbridge, hoping it might catch their tail. No such luck. The car kept up with him. But in the distance, a siren wailed. Help was on the way.

The car sped up again, rammed into his side and sent his car skidding sideways. He lost control, tires screeched and the car nosedived into the inlet. Water began rising, the car sinking deeper and deeper.

"Get out!" he barked.

Stella tried to open the door, but it was stuck in the sludge.

He yanked at his own, but like hers, the door was wedged deep into the wet earth. They were trapped. He tried the automatic window buttons but the windows refused to budge.

Stella's panicked gaze met his. Another shot hit the roof of the car.

He jerked his jacket from the back, wrapped it around his fist and smashed his window, hitting it over and over, targeting the edges now to free the jagged glass as water gushed inside the car.

"Come on!" He crawled through the opening, dove

into the water, then held out his hand to help Stella. She slid through the window, sank beneath the surface, then broke, gasping for air.

He motioned for her to stay low, then they ducked beneath the surface again and swam along the embankment. He thought his lungs would explode before he surfaced, and when he did, Stella was nowhere to be seen. But a red swirl of blood coated the water in front of him.

Had Stella been shot?

Rage and fear knifed through him. He dove under the water again to search for her.

STELLA SANK deeper and deeper below the surface of the water. Her lungs felt tight, the effort not to breathe taxing her. Darkness swirled around her, empty, never ending. She was so disoriented. Didn't know where she was going. Which direction to swim.

Tread water. Do whatever you have to do. Just keep yourself alive.

But her arms ached, her left one throbbing. The undertow sucked at her feet, pulling harder. Deeper. Like quicksand, it wouldn't release her.

She closed her eyes, then blinked to orient herself. She couldn't breathe. She couldn't see. It was so dark, the light extinguished forever.

Suddenly she was somewhere else. Lost in her memories.

HOW LONG HAD she been in the dark? How many days had they left her here alone?

And when they returned, what would they do to her this time?

Give her more shock treatments. Turn up the heat until her body shriveled up and withered away. Until she'd perspired so much she could no longer sweat. Until her lips stuck together, and she could no longer beg for water.

Or for her mother.

Maybe it was better if she gave up. Let them kill her. Then she wouldn't be forced to do those awful things.

Vile acts she'd refused to commit in the beginning. But they'd beaten her down. Driven her into submission. She couldn't fight their control any longer. Her mommy was never coming back. And the others…their eyes were so empty. Their bodies tortured just like hers. The cries she used to hear at night fading into acceptance.

Then she saw the fire. Cutting through the dark. Eating at her feet. The devil's hands reached for her.

She latched onto his hand.

No, she had to escape. Free herself. But there was no way out. No escape. Nothing but pain and whispers of evil.

She had to follow his commands.

Then another devil stood before her. This man prepared to kill her. She aimed the gun and fired…saw the man's face in death. His bloody body.

The Master would be pleased. Wouldn't punish her tonight.

But there was always tomorrow…

It would never end. It would start all over again in the morning. The pain. The isolation. The emptiness.

The unknown horrors.

Unless she ended it herself.

She closed her eyes, opened her mouth, drank in the salty water and braced herself to die. Death was the only way to stop the torture….

LUKE SEARCHED frantically for Stella, breaking only long enough to drag in a gulp of air. Thankfully he didn't hear the shooters any longer, but what had happened to Stella? She couldn't be dead.

His heart pounding, he dove beneath the murky water, wishing like hell it wasn't so damn black. He swam deeper, turning in circles, pedaling his arms as he swam further out from the shore. The tide was going out. What if the undertow had carried her out to sea?

Plowing on at least another quarter mile, he finally spotted her gun against a rock. Stella had to be close by. He swam faster. A few feet away, Stella's body sank deeper and deeper toward the bottom. He broke into a fast underwater swim, fighting the waves until he reached her. Bubbles floated upward, alerting him to the fact that she was in trouble.

He grabbed her and swam upward, kicking frantically, his pulse accelerating at the sight of the blood seeping from her arm. Finally, he broke the surface, gulped in air, then secured one arm around her and swam toward the embankment. Another couple of minutes and he dragged her onto the bank, laid her on the grassy slope and checked to see if she was breathing.

No.

Dear God.

He tilted her head back, cleared her air passage, pinched her nose and began CPR, counting and breathing in and out for her, praying at the same time. Ten-

sion swirled around him, the waves crashing below reminding him that another few seconds, and he would
have been too late.

"Come on, Stella, dammit, you can't die on me." He
performed another set of compressions, then breathed
into her mouth one more time, pulling back to check
her reaction. A heartbeat later, she coughed and began
to spit up. He sighed with relief, and tilted her head
sideways until she purged herself of the salty water.

"God, Stella, you scared the life out of me."

She gasped and choked again, tears streaming down
her face as he dragged her into his arms and rocked her.

Minutes ticked by as they held on to each other, her
sobs escalating as he cradled her closer.

"You should have let me die," she whispered.

His chest squeezed at her tortured words. "Shh, don't
say that."

"It's true. You don't know everything, you should
have let me die. Then it would be over."

"What would be over?"

"The pain," she cried. "Sutton would be gone, and
you would be safe…."

He cupped her face into one hand and angled her
chin up to look into her eyes, her comment moving
something deep inside him.

"I didn't deserve to be saved," she said in an an-
guished whisper.

"Don't talk like that, Stella. You're delirious." He
glanced at the embankment, hoping backup had caught
the car that had hit them as he grabbed his phone to call
for an ambulance.

She clutched his arm in panic. "What are you doing?"

"Calling an ambulance."

"No, no hospitals." She shoved at his shoulders, but he held her securely. She had a fear of hospitals, he realized, remembering the night he'd arranged for the exam. And when he'd seen her in the prison the next morning…had her reaction been due to the confinement or the hospital visit? What exactly had happened to Stella?

"Please," she whispered. "I'm okay now. It's just a scrape. I don't need to go to a hospital."

He studied her face. Decided that if Sutton were behind the shooting and their accident, he'd probably check there anyway. A safe house might be better.

"I'll call Detective Black then. He'll help us."

She frowned, and he realized he'd used the term to refer to both of them, as if they were together in this. It was true. He was crossing the line now. Something he'd vowed never to do.

But he couldn't leave Stella. Had known the minute he'd found her again that he wouldn't stop until he unraveled the entire truth.

The phone was dead, so he ran to the road and flagged down a trucker. The big, burly man handed Luke his cell immediately. Luke dialed Detective Black and explained the situation. "Did you catch the shooter?"

"No, sorry, we lost the car, but I've called in other units, maybe they'll spot the guy."

Luke grimaced.

"Are you all right?" Black asked. "Do you need an E.M.T.?"

"No, we're okay. We just need a ride."

"I'll be right there," Black said.

Luke hung up, then cradled Stella closer and checked her wound. "We'll go to a safe house. Once you're rested, we'll talk."

She nodded, then closed her eyes and gave in to the exhaustion. He held her tightly in his arms, his thoughts scattered. What was he going to do now?

In spite of his reservations, the answer came to him. He'd protect Stella from Sutton or whoever else was after her. And he'd track down the person responsible for trying to kill them tonight, and learn the truth about her past.

Then he vowed to get vengeance on the man who'd tried to kill her.

BY THE TIME Black arrived, Stella had fallen into a deep, troubled sleep. Luke carried her to Detective Black's car, slid inside and held her in his lap.

"Does she need a doctor?"

"Probably," Luke said. "But she refuses medical care. I'll find a safe place for the night and watch over her."

Black chewed the inside of his cheek. "Are you sure that's smart, Devlin? We both know Spencer is concerned about your objectivity."

"She's my wife, dammit." Luke grimaced and brushed a strand of damp hair from her face. "I know she lied, that she's not what she first appeared to be, so I'm not wearing blinders. But something else is going on."

Black remained silent for a moment, then finally replied, "All right. I know a place." Black veered onto the road and headed in the opposite direction toward Skidaway island. "What do you mean about something else going on?"

He explained about the ambush. "Stella muttered some odd things back there. I think her memories may be surfacing."

"And you believe she'll confide in you even though she's aware you're committed to the bureau."

Luke nodded. Was he as committed as Black thought? As he'd thought himself? Just how far would he cross the line for Stella?

"I need time to talk to her," Luke said.

"You mean an interrogation?" Black cut him a small smile.

Luke nodded, grateful for Black's leeway.

"I can give you that," Black said. "But keep me posted."

"Thanks, Detective. I owe you one."

"Don't make me regret it," Black said. "But for what it's worth, I understand what it's like."

"What do you mean?"

"To fall for a woman who's in trouble." He lifted his hand and Luke saw the wedding band glinting in the light. "I'd do anything for my wife and baby," he said. "Anything at all."

Luke glanced down at Stella. Saw her face twist in anguish. Remembered her plea that she should have died. Wondered what kind of nightmares were tormenting her now. What kind had tormented her the last year. And maybe her entire life.

Something bad had happened to Stella to bring her to this point.

And he would find out what that was. And if Sutton were behind it, he'd kill the bastard for hurting her.

STELLA ROUSED from sleep as Luke laid her on a bed. "Where are we?"

"A safe house. It's a cabin on Skidaway Island."

"They'll find us."

"No, no one knows we're here. We can get some rest. Regroup in the morning."

She nodded, hugging her arms to herself. She was so wet and cold. Troubling memories bombarded her. Going for days without food. Without water or sleep. Lying in the dark. Alone.

Never knowing if anyone would come for her.

And then the pain…

"Shh." Luke brushed her hair from her face. Wiped a tear from her cheek when she didn't even realize she'd been crying. "We have to remove these wet clothes," he murmured.

She struggled to keep her eyes open. Although it was hot outside, her teeth were chattering. And she was trembling all over.

Luke removed her blouse, her pants, her underwear came next. She felt so vulnerable. Then she realized he was getting naked, too. He was going to make love to her.

A sweet euphoria washed over her. She reached for him as he slid beneath the covers beside her. He cradled her in his arms, pulled her up next to his warm body. Her arms slid around his waist, her head found his broad shoulder as a pillow. His coarse chest hair brushed her cheek. Felt heavenly.

She stroked his back, felt the muscles bunch and contract. Lifted her lips to plant soft kisses against his neck.

"Shh, go back to sleep, Stella."

She nodded against him, fatigue already dragging her back into a deep sleep. But she wanted Luke. Needed him closer. Craved his loving touches. His kisses and hands exploring her. Ached to have him inside her.

She slid one hand lower.

"Stella, you need to rest." He rolled her away from him, then spooned her, his arms holding her securely in his embrace. Stella smiled into the pillow. She'd never had a man hold her with such tenderness.

Giving in to the sweet sensation, she closed her eyes and drifted to sleep, dreaming of tomorrow. This one filled with hope, not despair. And the promise of making love with Luke.

But soon the nightmares began.

And she was telling Luke the truth, at least parts that she could remember. This time he wasn't holding her or making love. Instead he carted her back to jail to be locked up like an animal.

And then he left her alone…

IT TOOK EVERY OUNCE of Luke's restraint not to make love to Stella. He wanted her with an intensity that frightened him.

But he'd already crossed the line tonight. He should have called his superior.

Spencer doesn't trust you.

And hiding Stella like this would only make him appear guilty of crossing over.

If he made love to her tonight, there was no going back. He'd completely lose his objectivity.

Questions tormented him during the long restless night, just as Stella's nightmares tortured her.

"No, so cold. Need light." She moaned and clutched at his arms, trembling anew. "No more darkness."

He hugged her closer, rocking her gently until she settled back down. But other murmurings drifted from her lips during the night. More comments that sounded like agony.

He swallowed hard, hating the images that flashed in his head. And when morning slashed through the windows, bringing the first strains of daylight, he knew Stella's nightmares were very real. Memories, not dreams.

She scooted closer to him, seemed to melt into his body. Other emotions stirred inside him. Protective feelings he shouldn't allow.

Arousal pulsed through him, too. His sex hardened, the feel of her naked body brushing his another kind of torment. When she rolled over and opened her eyes, the sultry sleepy look of a hungry woman, he finally relented, bowed his head and kissed her.

One kiss nearly sent his world spinning. She slid a hand into his hair, pulled him closer. Her taut nipples stabbed at his chest, begging for touches. He obliged, stroking and rubbing. Her leg slipped between his, her foot massaging his calf, her sex brushing his in a sensual game of male meets female.

He teased her lips apart with his tongue, delving inside to taste her. She sighed and ran her hands over his chest, around to his back, gyrating her body toward him, fitting herself so his erection throbbed against her thigh. He cupped her breast in one hand, the other lowering to tease her lips apart, probe her wetness. His heart pounding, he suckled her breasts, first one, then the other, savoring her reaction.

He had to have more. Had to taste her everywhere. He dipped his head lower, licked a path down her body. Spread her legs and placed his tongue where his fingers had been, to the heart of her. She bucked upward, clawing at the sheets, moaning his name as her wetness filled his mouth.

Then she flipped him over. Reversed the positions. Slid lower. Kissed his chest. Licked her way to his navel. Her hand cupped his sex and stroked his hardness. Her mouth came nearer.

When he realized her intention, he froze. Realized what he was doing.

Crossing the line even further. Breaking his own promise.

He pushed her hand away, lifted her gently. "No, Stella."

A stunned, almost hurt look flickered in her eyes when she looked up at him. He almost relented.

But if he did, he'd never be able to release her. Never know the truth.

If she were seducing him for deceptive reasons.

"I want to give you pleasure," she whispered.

Heaven help him, she was a vixen.

"Not now."

"But why?" she whispered. "You saved my life, Luke. You took care of me." She traced a finger over the damp moisture on the tip of his sex.

He shuddered, then gripped her shoulders, drawing on restraint he didn't even know he possessed. "I don't want to have sex with you, Stella, as some kind of payment. I want it to be more."

Her face flushed crimson. "I didn't mean it like that."

He swallowed, still so tempted. Why did he feel this intensely urgent pull toward her, when with other women, he'd been void of emotion?

But everything was different with Stella.

He brushed the back of his hand down her cheek tenderly. "I have a feeling people have been taking from you all your life, using you, Stella. I don't want that." He stood, his sex throbbing, pulsing toward her. His heart squeezed. "When we make love again, and we will make love," he said in a gruff voice, "I don't want lies or secrets between us. I want you completely."

SUTTON PACED his study, gripped the phone in one hand while he poured himself a third scotch and downed it. His boss had been on a tirade for half an hour.

"What the hell is going on with the Segall woman?"

"I thought I had her under control." But the call from Jaycee and Kat had proven differently. And now Stella had disappeared with Luke Devlin.

"It certainly doesn't sound that way."

Fury rolled through him. He gripped the highball glass so hard it shattered. Blood trickled down his palm onto the oriental rug.

He grabbed a handkerchief and wrapped his hand quickly. The rug was a piece of art. He couldn't ruin it.

Just like he couldn't let Stella ruin the project.

"She's been a loose cannon for a long time. We should have eliminated her when we erased the others."

Sutton's chest constricted, and he reached for the scotch bottle again. Stella had always been his favorite. Once upon a time, he'd had her under his thumb. She'd followed his every command. She'd been like a daughter.

Then her memories had started returning. And the blasted questions.

"You have to erase her," the Master said. "We can't afford for her to ruin our Nighthawk Island setup."

"The past will stay buried," Sutton assured him.

"It had better," the man growled. "Now bury the woman and that agent while you're at it."

Chapter Nine

Stella hugged the covers to her as Luke stalked into the bathroom and turned on the shower. She had never imagined him saying no to her. And not because he didn't want her, but because he did—*completely.*

A shiver traveled up her spine. Could she possibly give herself to a man completely?

Luke didn't know what he was asking. Totally giving herself meant she would have to trust him. Relinquish her power. Be submissive again.

A position she had vowed never again to place herself in.

A sudden realization dawned on her. She had been trying to escape Sutton a year ago and had turned to Luke to help her. She didn't recall all the details, but she had been fighting against Sutton's control.

Although, Luke hadn't meant his comment in the same way. He didn't want control. Instead he wanted her heart and soul.

That was even more scary. It meant telling him the truth. Confessing her sinful secrets. Exposing her vulnerablities.

Remembering things she'd shut out because they were too horrible to face.

And if she did admit the ugly truth, he wouldn't want her...

He was a lawman, a man of honor. A man who'd given her pleasure without taking his own.

When all Sutton had done was take from her. First her childhood. Then her willpower. Even her desire to live.

The shower door opened, steam oozing out, and Luke appeared with a towel wrapped around his waist. Moisture still dotted his dark chest, and his black hair was tousled and wet. A savage hunger rose inside her. She wanted to run her hands through his hair. All over his body. Strip the towel and make love to him.

I want you completely.

But she wasn't ready for that.

"The bathroom's yours," he said in a gruff voice.

A raw primal need flared in his eyes while he waited for her response. But Stella couldn't relinquish control.

She stood, wrapped the sheet around her and walked into the bathroom. Twenty minutes later she emerged, her body still aching with want. He had apparently laid a pair of loose warm up pants and a T-shirt on the bed for her, so she slipped them on and went to the kitchen.

Already dressed, Luke handed her a cup of coffee.

"Thanks." She indicated the T-shirt and warm-up pants. "Where did you get the clothes?"

"The locals have used this place as a safe house before. They keep it stocked with a few basic things."

She nodded and sipped the coffee, her gaze drawn to his mouth as he drank his own.

"Stop looking at me like that, Stella."

A small smile quirked her mouth. With his hair still damp, he looked delicious. "Like what?"

His eyes darkened. "You know."

She smiled, and sank into the kitchen chair. "I can't help it. I've never had a man treat me like you did earlier."

This time he smiled, his own look of hunger deepening. Obviously determined to maintain control, he closed his eyes, swallowed another sip of coffee, then looked at her again, his expression serious. "Your memories are returning, aren't they?"

"I think so, but they're all jumbled." She set the mug down, traced a finger around the edge. "It's hard for me to tell what's real and what isn't. Some of my visions…they might just be nightmares."

"Ones that really happened?"

She stared into her coffee. "Maybe."

"Why don't you tell me about them. Maybe we can make sense of them together."

She contemplated her choices. "If I tell you, you'll never look at me the same way again. Never…"

"Never want you?"

She nodded, her throat clogging with emotions.

"Do you really care what I think, Stella?" Luke asked.

"Yes," she whispered. "I think I always have."

"Then trust me not to let your past affect me." He tilted her chin up. "No matter what happens between us, you're not going back to Sutton."

No, she couldn't do that. "But you want to put me in jail. And I'll die if you do that, Luke. I…can't ever go back. Be locked up. Caged like an animal."

"You've been in prison before?"

She shook her head. "Not that kind of jail."

He gritted his teeth. "I...maybe we can work something out, Stella. If you help me, that is."

She sighed. "You mean like the witness protection program?"

He shrugged. "It's a possibility."

She contemplated the thought. Under the program, she could assume a new identity. Start over.

Erase her past. Have a new life. Literally become another person.

But that would also mean severing all ties with Luke. Then she'd be all alone.

"I just want the truth," Luke said.

"But what if the answers I give you aren't what you want to hear?" Stella whispered.

"I'm a big boy." He circled the table, knelt and cradled her hands in his. "I've been an agent a long time, Stella. I've seen things that I don't like to talk about, things that...give me nightmares. I promise I'll try to understand."

Riveted by his words, she stared into his eyes, wanting to believe him, but so afraid.

"What does Sutton want with you? Is he in love with you?"

"No. It's not about sex."

He hesitated. "Then what?"

"Ownership."

His jaw tightened.

"Controlling me," she admitted. "Kat. Jaycee."

"Who are Jaycee and Kat?"

"Two of the others." She licked her dry lips. "I...you know already don't you?"

"That you were involved in espionage? Yes."

She sank lower into despair. "Then why the questions, Luke? Why not just arrest me for being a traitor? Lock me up and throw away the key?"

"Because there's more to the story. First, I don't think that you're the leader, and that's who we really want." He rubbed his hands over hers, warming them. "I'm not sure you were fully aware of all your actions, either. You were definitely coerced."

"Don't make excuses for me, Luke. I won't." But her nightmare returned. *Do as he says. Submit. Follow his commands or be punished.*

She didn't realize she'd voiced the thoughts out loud until Luke's sharp intake of air broke the silence. She looked into his eyes. Saw the disgust.

And turned away.

But he spun her back around, forcing her to look at him. "What else, Stella? What did Sutton do to you? What do you remember?"

"I'm not sure," she whispered. "I only see bits and pieces. Some of them don't make sense."

He nodded. "What about last week? What happened at his house?"

She chewed on bottom lip. "He took me to a suite upstairs in the house and locked me inside."

"You weren't free to move around the house?"

"No. A nurse monitored me daily. She also gave me injections." She rolled her arm over, showed him the marks.

"What kind of drugs?"

"I don't know. She insisted the doctor ordered the medication to help me rest. But it made me sleep all the time. I had nightmares and heard voices, even saw things."

"A hallucination?"

"I think so, although they could have been memories." She tightened her fingers inside his. "I finally asked them to stop. Told them the drugs made me groggy. That I wanted to wake up and know what was going on."

"Did they do as you asked?"

"Not at first. Then you showed up."

"Thank God," he murmured. A heartbeat of silence stretched between them. "Tell me about the bits and pieces of the memories. Everything, even the hallucinations."

She closed her eyes, images flooding her, and finally allowed the words to flow.

LUKE BRACED HIMSELF for Stella's story. He'd promised her he'd listen, that he wouldn't judge. He just hoped he could keep that promise.

But the thought of someone, especially Sutton, forcing her to obey him, sent a sour feeling to Luke's stomach.

"Sometimes I dream I'm a little girl," she said in a strained voice. "I'm on a cot in a room with other children. I'm crying for my mother and wondering where she is. I think they took her away, but they say she's dead."

"Who are *they?*"

She shook her head. "I…don't know. Sutton. The other men." She hesitated. "The other girls whisper that I have to forget my mother. And when I look at them, their expressions are so empty." She hesitated, her chin wobbling. "Then sometimes the men come and take us away. One at a time."

"How are they dressed? In military uniforms? As doctors?"

She froze. "They're wearing lab coats. White, like doctors."

Luke nodded. "What happens next, Stella?"

A glazed look filled her eyes. "I can't remember the details. But it's painful. They attach probes to me. Sometimes I feel sharp jolts of pain like shock waves. Sometimes I'm drugged and disoriented. And then there are dark voices."

Bile rose to Luke's throat at the thought of the frightened children. What exactly had Sutton been up to? "What else, Stella?"

"As I grow older, I'm locked in a tiny room for days. I can't even see my own hands it's so dark. Sometimes forced to do without water. Or food. Or light. Sometimes they show me pictures of people dying. I hear sounds of guns firing, over and over." Her hand trembled as she tucked her hair behind her ear. "Then I see the children. I'm one of them, and we're shooting. Being ordered to kill people. Late one night there was an explosion and fire. I see the flames eating up the floor. The blaze is all around me—" Her voice broke. "Then this man came in and reached for me. I hated him, but I went anyway."

"Was it Sutton?"

"I think so." She rubbed her hands up and down her arms. "I was so scared…."

"You're safe now, Stella." Sweat beaded his forehead as he stroked her hands in his.

She nodded. "But I knew he was the devil, and I went with him anyway."

Luke wasn't sure whether to believe her story so readily, but the anguish in her eyes seemed so real. "You were a child. You weren't to blame, Stella. You did what you had to do to survive."

She gazed into his eyes. Her terror appeared to run so deep that he pulled her into his arms and held her.

Or was he being a sucker again? He'd have to look further into her story. Still, if her memories were real, she'd endured something unconscionable, and he couldn't resist comforting her. "It takes strength to endure what you described and survive."

"I'm not strong. I was weak. I gave in—"

"You're only human, sweetheart. They took advantage of your age. They found your breaking point. Everyone has one."

"Sometimes at night, I hear this voice commanding me to do bad things," she said against his shoulder.

He stiffened slightly. Now she sounded schizophrenic.

"I have to follow his command. I have to…kill somebody. But…I don't want to do it anymore. I never wanted to."

He contemplated her admission. "I've heard of brainwashing techniques in other countries," Luke said. "But not in the States. That doesn't mean it didn't exist years ago, or that it isn't being done today behind closed doors." He stroked her hair, felt her tears dampen his shirt, wished he could alleviate the pain and horror of her past. "The man in the hotel—who was he?"

She blinked, then bit down on her lip. "Sutton said he was my handler. That he was going to expose us."

"Expose who? You, Sutton, Kat and Jaycee?"

She nodded and pulled away slightly, palming the tears from her cheeks. "Sutton has a secret room in the basement that's accessible through his study. There's an elaborate computer set up down there complete with surveillance equipment."

"And your mission was to meet me so you could get information on me?"

She nodded slowly.

"You were supposed to seduce me?"

She closed her eyes. "He wants information—it doesn't matter how the agent obtains it."

"So, the marriage was a sham."

She looked up at him, winced, then shook her head. "I think it started that way, but I…later, I was trying to escape from Sutton."

He stewed that over for a minute. Wanted to believe her. His FBI instincts warned him not to trust anything she said though.

But the male side of him, the part of him that had held her, that was looking into her troubled eyes and that'd just heard her story, swung the other way on the pendulum.

He forced himself not to respond either way. Couldn't yet. Not until he knew more, and had more time to watch Stella. "What information did Sutton want you to extract from me?"

She hesitated, seemed to accept his silence with resignation.

That alone nearly broke his resolve. He sensed Stella had been forced to accept a world of distrust early on.

That she'd never known any different. Men using her. Abusing her.

Being abandoned.

Her soft labored sigh drew his attention. "He knew you were investigating the projects on Nighthawk Island."

"Did he mention any specific project?"

"No."

Quinn's undercover position came to mind. "I'll have to talk to…my contacts," Luke said, catching himself. Sutton was smart. As much as he wanted to believe Stella and trust her, if Sutton got her again and tortured her, any information he confided in her might end up with Sutton. Luke couldn't afford to blow Quinn's cover and endanger him.

Now came another hard question. The one he already knew the answer to, but had to ask anyway. "What were you doing at my cabin last night?"

She flinched, slowly dropping her head forward so a curtain of hair shielded her eyes. "Sutton told me that a reporter sent you a disk containing incriminating evidence against me. I was suppose to retrieve it."

Luke silently cursed. In the haste of the shooting last night and in his hurry to rush Stella to safety after that dive into the ocean, he'd forgotten about the disk. And how did Sutton know the reporter had contacted him? Two possibilities. One, Sutton had a tap on his phone. Two, the reporter was working both sides. "Did you find the disk?"

She shook her head.

"And you were supposed to take it back to Sutton?"

She nodded. "And then…" She raised her head, looked straight at him, a torn look in her eyes. "I was supposed to kill you."

STELLA WINCED at her own admission. But there, she'd said it. Luke had either figured out the truth himself, or he was trying to ring a confession from her, and she'd just walked into the trap.

At this point, she wasn't sure it mattered.

Unless he broke his promise and sent her to jail.

"But you couldn't shoot me, could you, Stella?"

His husky voice sent her nerves into a tailspin. She had pulled the gun, pointed it at him, but her hand trembled. She'd started to lower the weapon when he'd lunged toward her, and the bullets had started flying. "No."

He squeezed her hand again. "I have to talk to that reporter. See what's on that disk."

She nodded.

"But I need to make a couple of phone calls first. Verify that Sutton isn't monitoring my calls. Check on my contact at Nighthawk Island." He stood, poured himself another cup of coffee and strode into the den for privacy. She warmed her own cup, uncertain where they went from here.

But she wouldn't return to Sutton's. Not ever again.

The memory of that little girl crying for her mother flashed back, and Stella struggled to recall more details. How had she come to be at that dormitory with the other girls? She'd asked that question over and over, but the answer had always been the same. Sutton had insisted her parents had died.

But Sutton was ruthless. He could have lied to her. Had he killed her mother instead?

"QUINN, BE CAREFUL." Luke stared out the window as he gripped the phone handset. "Someone may be on you tail."

"Don't worry, I can handle it," Quinn replied. "Remember I was in special ops."

"Have you noticed any research that raises a red flag?" Luke asked.

"A couple, but I don't have anything concrete. One of the major projects involves stem cells. And they're researching biological and chemical warfare, although information is dispensed on a need-to-know basis. Security is tight. There's another study focusing on cloning and one on face transplants."

"Face transplants?"

"Yes, from cadavers. Burn patients, accident victims, people born with terrible birth defects—they would benefit."

Luke grimaced. Some would take it farther. Choose a face as a new disguise. He could see the possibilities for the witness protection program.

But would others want to use it to replace plastic surgery?

"See what you can find on an experiment that took place fifteen to twenty years ago involving children," Luke said. "The subjects might have been orphans or kidnap victims. Brainwashing techniques such as sensory deprivation were probably used. I think the subjects might have been trained as covert agents."

"You're kidding, right?"

"Hell, I wish I was."

Quinn hesitated. "Does this involve your wife?"

Luke spared Stella a glance, the pain in her eyes ripping at him. "Yes, she was one of the children."

Quinn cursed. "I'll see what I can dig up."

Luke thanked him, hung up, phoned Detective Black, and relayed what he'd learned from Stella.

Black grunted. "Man, Sutton is one cold son of a bitch."

"That's putting it mildly."

"How's Stella?"

"I think she's suffering from Post Traumatic Syndrome," Luke said. "She's having nightmares, some memories are returning, but they're all jumbled and confused."

"She admitted to killing the man?" Black asked.

Luke considered a lie, but he'd sworn to be straight with Black, and he never broke his word. Besides, under the circumstances, he was certain he could arrange a deal for Stella, providing she testified against Sutton.

"Devlin?"

"She doesn't exactly remember firing the gun, but she admitted she was supposed to kill him. He was her handler and had planned to expose her."

"What about the drugs in her system? She could have blacked out."

"My thoughts exactly. Perhaps Sutton framed her because she tried to escape. When she stayed with him the past few days, he ordered a nurse to drug her." Luke paused. "I'll check my house for that disk that Andrews was supposed to send over." Although the shooters might have already taken it. "Did you get CSI to process my place?"

"Yeah. They're testing the bullets they found now."

"Good. Let me know if they find any prints."

Black agreed, and promised to meet Luke at the morgue. Luke made another phone call to the bureau to verify that Sutton couldn't monitor his calls, then hung up and turned to Stella. "Are you ready to take a ride?"

Fear flashed in her eyes. She obviously wondered if he intended to keep his word about not taking her back to prison. She still didn't trust him.

"Where are we going?" she asked.

"To my cabin to find that disk. And if it's not there, we'll visit that reporter, Andrews. I want to find out exactly what he knows." He hesitated. "But we have to stop by the morgue first. The coroner's ready to release the information on Raul Jarad's autopsy."

DR. YATES, the medical examiner, showed Luke and Stella to his office. Seconds later, Detectives Black and Fox joined them.

Dr. Yates motioned for the men to follow.

Stella hung back. "Should I come?"

"No," Luke answered. "Wait here."

She nodded, and took a seat in the office, while Luke followed Black and Fox.

"Cause of death was a bullet wound to the head," Dr. Yates said. "We retrieved the bullet, and I've sent it to ballistics."

"Any other wounds on the body?" Luke asked.

"Bruises. Some old, some new. He has a lot of scarring, too." Dr. Yates turned the body so they could see his back. "These appear to be burn marks." He indicated a few other scars which looked suspicious. Some to his feet and hands.

"I thought this was odd, too." Dr. Yates indicated a small mark behind the man's ear. "Look at this carving, it's like a tattoo or burn, triangular shaped. I've never seen anything quite like it."

It reminded Luke of a prison or gang tattoo, or perhaps a prisoner of war marking.

He remembered Stella's scattered memories of her youth and wondered if this man had been part of some kind of experiment or brainwashing technique as well.

He'd have to probe Stella further.

In fact, maybe he should have Stella view Jarad's body and watch her reaction.

STELLA'S NERVES ping-ponged between nausea and disbelief as she stared at Raul Jarad. Sutton had claimed that Raul was her handler, that he was going to expose her. So why did she have this uncanny sense of sadness as she looked at his face?

Luke pressed a hand to her back. "Do you remember him?"

She experienced a brief flash of the two of them on a mission, shooting and covering for one another. But as quickly as the image came, it faded. "Not really."

"He died from the gunshot to the head," Luke said. "The bullet's in ballistics."

"You know it'll match the gun I was holding."

Luke shrugged. "Probably." He escorted her outside, then hesitated as if he wanted to say more.

"What is it, Luke?"

"Jarad had an odd marking behind his ear." He gently lifted the hair from Stella's neck and checked behind it. She definitely had a scar, but the marking was different.

"What is it, Luke?"

"You have one, too, but it's a number," he said quietly. He couldn't believe he'd never noticed it before. But it was so tiny it was almost indistinguishable.

"A number?"

He nodded. "My guess is it had something to do with those memories of yours. Of being given shock treatment, and undergoing sensory deprivation experiments."

"I was a number in an experiment?" She fought the idea, although other brief snippets of her past flashed back. The girls lined up. Their numbers being called. Being divided into sections.

Luke stroked her back slowly. "Come on, let's look for that disk. Maybe it will provide us with the answers."

She nodded, struggling to fill in the blanks, but once again, the curtain closed on her memories.

The ride passed in virtual silence. Stella regarded the beautiful serenity of Skidaway with envy, willing the peaceful atmosphere to tame the anxiety riddling her. A deer hesitated at the sound of their car rumbling by, perked its ears and stared at them but didn't move. A fawn loped up beside it, nudging its mother. Her throat swelled as she watched the pair together, their trust of the environment and people on the island evident. The land was well preserved, its natural habitat and terrain undisturbed save for the occasional house or subdivision which had apparently been built to code to glorify nature, not destroy it.

How odd that the animals that should be defensive of strangers trusted so easily when she herself couldn't.

Of course, she didn't remember ever feeling safe…

You were a number. Not even human.

Luke parked in front of his cabin, and they hurried inside to search for the disk. An hour later, they'd come up empty, so they headed to Andrews's place.

Luke turned onto the road leading to Savannah, then veered onto a side street leading to an older development. A few houses, mostly wooden and weathered were scattered through the marshy area.

Luke checked the address, maneuvered another turn, then followed a road which seemed uninhabited. A few hundred feet away, smoke plumes floated upward.

Luke sped up, and Stella leaned forward to search through the thick, heavy, black smoke.

"Damn."

"What is it?" Stella asked.

"That's Andrews's house." He screeched to a halt at the end of the driveway, then tossed her the new phone the Feds had given him. "Call 911, then Detective Black at the police station!"

"Wait, Luke, where are you going?"

"To see if Andrews is inside."

He vaulted from the car and took off running.

Stella punched in the emergency number, her heart in her throat as fire shot into the sky, and Luke darted directly into it.

Chapter Ten

Stella called 911 as fire crackled and popped, and wood exploded. Part of the roof caved in, and Stella screamed and raced toward the house. "Luke!"

The front porch completely erupted in flames. Heat seared Stella's face and arms as she approached, thick black smoke curling and rising toward the heavens. She ran to the back to see if there was another entrance, but flames clawed at the floor and walls there, blocking her way. Panicked, she darted to the side window and glanced inside, searching desperately for Luke. More flames crawled along the den carpet toward the hall, patches of bright orange fireballs bursting in front of her eyes.

Once again the memories of her childhood flooded her.

SHE WAS TRAPPED. Caught in the bed in the long dormitory room. It had been so dark before, and cold, but now fire scalded her face and hands, and lit the darkness. The bright yellow and orange flames rose around her, dancing toward her, burning the bedspread that had fallen to the floor. She climbed toward the top of the bed to escape.

From their beds, Nadine and Bianca cried and

screamed. But the fire was already licking their sheets. Nadine batted at it with her pillow. Bianca was coughing and choking, jumping up and down to dodge the flames as they drew closer and closer.

"Take my hand, Stella. Come on, I'm going to save you."

She saw the man. His dark hair. Those soulless eyes. He was reaching for her. And so was the fire. She lurched for him, knowing he was the devil. But she had to save herself.

Just then the fire exploded around Nadine.

"No!" Stella screamed and cried, yelled at the man to save them.

He jerked the sheet off her bed, wrapped it around her, then ran for the door, hauling her to his side as he sidestepped the fire. She scratched and pounded at his arms to go back and save Nadine and Bianca, but he raced through the hallways, not even looking back. Metal and wood exploded around her. Terrified screams mingled with the shattering wood. Cries of pain and death.

Another man appeared in the smoke-filled distance. The Master they called him.

A real-life monster.

A shrill scream pierced the air. Stella covered her ears to drown out the sounds. She was sobbing uncontrollably. She should have told the man to get Nadine and Bianca first. That she would follow.

Now they couldn't make it out. And it was her fault...

A SIREN WAILED in the distance, louder, closer. Stella jerked from the memories. The ambulance was coming to save Luke. They had to be in time.

Just like years ago with the other girls, she had been too much of a coward to do so herself.

LUKE FOUND an afghan on the floor and used it to bat at the flames and help protect himself from inhaling the smoke as he darted through the house. Fire and heat seared his back, feet and arms as he dodged the worst of the blaze, and slithered between the patches of floor that hadn't yet caught ablaze.

Andrews wasn't in the den. The computer equipment was already melting and ruined, any papers or diskettes destroyed. The furniture was ablaze, and smoke filled the room and rippled through the house. A loud sound jolted him, and pieces of the ceiling crashed down around him. He jumped aside, but one caught him on the shoulder. He slapped at the fire eating at his sleeve and jogged through the hallway to the bedrooms.

Andrews wasn't inside the first bedroom. He checked the bathroom, and tub, but it was empty, too. More of the roof crashed behind him, and he dashed to the last bedroom. Fire already seeped along the edges, consuming the curtains and old wooden dresser. He crouched low, covering his mouth and coughing, then blinked to clear his eyes from the fog of smoke. Seconds later, he spotted Andrews on the floor, unconscious.

He raced toward him and knelt, then checked for a pulse. He couldn't find one.

Knowing he had to start CPR, but not in the burning house, he dragged Andrews over his shoulder. The hallway was completely ablaze, the roof collapsing in sections like dominoes falling.

Heaving air, he threw the afghan over Andrews and searched for a back door, but the only way out was the window. Flames already encircled the glass, black curtain ashes raining down to the burning floor. He braced Andrews over his shoulder, then ran through the firey window, diving to the ground outside. The man's dead weight pummeled him as he collapsed.

A second later, Stella screamed his name.

"I'm out!" He rolled over, slapping at the flames on his boots, and saw her running toward him. The fire engine barreled into the drive. Firemen jumped from the truck and began to hose down the flames. It was too late to save the house, but they needed to keep the fire from spreading.

He reached under Andrews's arms and hauled him away from the flames.

"Luke!" Stella grabbed his arm. "Are you okay?"

Terror darkened her eyes as she clung to him. "I thought you were dead!"

He massaged her back to soothe her. "I'm okay. But get the paramedics!"

She nodded, brushed at her tears then ran toward the front to signal the rescue team while he knelt and checked for signs of life from Andrews.

Again, he couldn't find a pulse.

Then he noticed the gunshot wound in the man's temple.

It looked like a professional hit.

The paramedics rushed up, and he moved aside to give them access, but at the sight of the gunshot, they shook their heads. Luke pulled Stella into his arms and held her, trying to calm her. She was trembling, almost hysterical.

"Look at me, Stella, I'm fine." He forced her to look at him. She seemed dazed. Then he remembered the fire she'd described as a child, and understood her terror.

The police car arrived, and Detectives Black and Fox jumped out, joining them.

"What happened?" Black asked.

"The house was ablaze when we arrived," Luke said. "I found Andrews unconscious in the bedroom."

Fox walked over to the paramedic. "Is he going to make it?"

"No. He was probably dead before the fire started." While the paramedics retrieved the stretcher, Luke showed Fox the gunshot wound, then rolled the man's body over. Deep gashes marked Andrews's head as well as an exit wound for the bullet.

"We need a CSI team to go through the place," Fox said. "My guess is that bullet will match the ones from your cabin, Devlin."

Luke nodded and glanced down at Stella, who paled even more. She didn't ask any questions. She must have recognized the work.

They both knew who had probably done it.

But any information Andrews had obtained had died with him.

STELLA LISTENED quietly while Luke and the detectives discussed how best to handle the case.

"I think Sutton is responsible," Luke said. "But we need proof."

"You think this fire is connected to Nighthawk Island?" Black asked.

"Maybe. I also suspect it's connected to Stella and Sutton, and a research project that took place years ago."

"You can try questioning the director of CIRP, Ian Hall," Black said. "But I doubt you'll get very far. The doctors are extremely secretive and protective of their work at the research park."

"I know, but I'll pressure him," Luke said. "Maybe if I explain the circumstances, he'll cooperate."

Stella watched the flames die to embers as the firemen doused them with gallons of water. The charred remains reminded her of her own life, gray and ruined.

Drake Sutton was the one with answers, the one who had made her existence as dirty as those brittle ashes. She had to make him explain why he'd saved her and not the other girls.

And why he had saved her life only to turn her into a killer.

The answers were probably in that elaborate computer system in his basement. If only she could gain access to it. Maybe she could hack her way through and find out the truth. Discover a way to hang Sutton.

She contemplated various ideas while Luke met with the crime scene unit that arrived shortly after the firemen. Luke had resorted to all business. But occasionally, he shot her a concerned glance. Several times, she considered taking the car and driving to Sutton's. But she had to choose the right time.

Besides, Luke had almost died earlier. She wasn't ready to leave him, would blame herself if something happened to him.

Finally he approached her and climbed into the car. "We're going to meet Ian Hall, the Director of CIRP."

She nodded, and they rode to the facility on Catcall Island in silence. Soot and sweat stained Luke's face and shirt. The scent of smoke permeated the car, reminding her of his close call with death. The second since she'd resurfaced in his life.

Luke didn't deserve to die because of her.

Twenty minutes later, they were seated in Dr. Hall's office. Ian Hall was attractive, very well dressed, nice mannered, distinguished looking. But Stella didn't trust anyone, and wondered if his appearance and demeanor were simply a front.

"What can I do for you, Agent Devlin?"

Luke explained about the reporter's death and the circumstances leading to it. "We believe that Miss Segall was a victim of an experiment that was conducted about twenty-five years ago."

"As you know, I've only recently accepted the directorship role at CIRP," Hall stated. "I wouldn't have knowledge about something that happened that long ago." He steepled his hands. "I'm working diligently to earn a better reputation for the research facility."

"So I've heard. That's one reason I thought you might help us," Luke said smoothly. "I'd appreciate it if you'd look for any old files that might contain information about past research experiments using children as subjects. Perhaps some early brainwashing methods or programming techniques using sensory deprivation and shock therapy."

Hall swallowed, looking uncomfortable. "You believe someone brainwashed children—for what purpose?"

"To turn them into agents. Specifically, killers."

Hall's face blanched. "In all the work I've read about here, I know nothing of such a project. And I can assure you that if I had been in charge, irreputable project would never have been sanctioned."

Luke frowned. "Unfortunately you weren't around then, Dr. Hall. This experiment occurred during the Cold War. The climate was different at that time, government restrictions not as monitored." Luke hesitated, leaning forward. "You're aware of the unethical experiments and cover-ups that took place here before you came?"

When Hall conceded, Luke explained about Drake Sutton. "I don't think Sutton was in charge of the project, but believe he was and still is answering to a higher authority."

"I'll see what I can do, Agent Devlin." Dr. Hall stood and shook their hands, signaling the end of the meeting.

"How do you think that went?" Stella asked, as they exited the building.

Luke shrugged. "I didn't expect him to offer up anything directly. But if he's the good guy he's pretending to be, he'll check out my theory. If for no other reason than to avoid bad publicity for the research park."

Luke's cell phone rang, and he answered it, speaking in a hushed voice as he climbed into the car. Stella glanced at the research building again, then noticed someone staring at them from a top window above Ian Hall's office. When the person saw her looking at him, he flipped the blinds closed. A shiver raced through her. Someone had been watching them. Which meant that someone here at the research park knew why they'd come. Maybe they even had the answers to their questions.

Drake Sutton's face flashed into her mind. He had all the answers she wanted.

Like what had happened to her mother. And as soon as Luke left her alone for a minute, she intended to confront Sutton and force him to admit the truth.

LUKE LISTENED to Quinn Salt's findings in abject silence.

"I don't have all the answers yet," Agent Salt said. "But I discovered some old notes in a storage unit. There was a project named SHIP around the time you mentioned. Young children were forced to endure sensory deprivation as well as other torture. There has to be more details here somewhere, but I haven't located them yet."

"Were names mentioned?"

"No, everything was in code. It appears that the project might be related to another one involving genetic engineering to create a physically strong child, but one with with no emotion."

"They wanted to train the children as spies and agents. Without emotion, they could be hired killers."

Quinn grunted. "It's hard to believe a group like that existed twenty years ago."

Yet if they were right, Stella was a living example.

"Does the file list the names of the children or provide any personal information about them?"

"No, but I'll keep looking." Quinn hesitated. "You think Stella was part of this?"

Luke glanced at the woman he'd married, the one he'd half hated the last year for leaving him, and emotions welled in his chest. "Yes."

"Then she must have been tough to survive. You won't believe some of the stuff they did to these kids. Besides the sensory deprivation, they used mind games. Drugs. Solitary confinement. Shock treatments. They even used repetitive videos of murders and simulations of being killed themselves to desensitize them. The children were programmed at such a young age, it would be impossible for them to be normal or unscarred."

"Even if they were reintegrated into the real world? Given therapy?"

"It's a long shot. Essentially they created sociopathic behavior. Humans without a conscience."

Luke's chest constricted as he imagined Stella as a young child enduring torture. She seemed to have found a conscience, though—at least if her tears were any indication.

Then again, what if Quinn were right? A sociopath could act or pretend emotion without really feeling it. Could play a part and seduce a person or adapt another persona in a second.

The sense of trust that he'd begun to feel since he'd discovered Stella in his apartment wavered. What if Stella were incapable of changing? What if she had simply pretended she couldn't shoot him to seduce him into believing her?

What if she were still communicating with Sutton—feeding him information and keeping Luke occupied in order to disguise ulterior motives?

LUKE HAD WITHDRAWN from her. Stella felt the cold distance yawning wider between them as he drove back to the safe house. She had no idea what had happened to him or what information he'd gleaned on the phone, but he had been silent since.

"Who was that you talked to?" she asked, unable to stand the tension any longer.

"An inside contact," he replied curtly.

"Did he have information about me? Or about Drake Sutton?"

"He's confirmed that notes detailed a project years ago involving the type of brainwashing and sensory deprivation experiments that you described in your nightmares."

Stella shivered. So she hadn't been dreaming those horrid things. They had really happened.

Which meant the fire years ago was real, too, and that Sutton had left some of the others to die.

Anger and guilt filled her.

Shame followed. Now she understood why Luke was behaving so oddly. He knew the real Stella now. Probably pitied her.

Or maybe his contact had informed him that she was a cold-blooded killer.

He parked, scanned the outside, then climbed out and walked her to the door. When he entered, he motioned for her to remain in the den while he checked the other rooms.

"It's clear," he said when he returned.

"You look tired, Luke." She moved toward him and brushed at the sooty ashes staining his collar. "I was worried when you ran in to save Andrews."

He looked down into her eyes, but a mask shielded his emotions. "Stay here and rest, Stella. I have things to take care of."

"What kind of things?"

"Business." He didn't elaborate, simply walked to the door. "Lock the door behind me. And don't let anyone in. I won't be gone long."

She met his gaze as he handed her a small handgun. "This is for protection."

She nodded, wondering if Luke's offer meant he trusted her, then watched him go in silence, confused. Last night, he had almost made love to her, had told her he wanted her completely. Had he changed his mind after that phone call?

Or had he realized that she could never give all of herself to one man? Sex was one thing. Trust and love another.

Damn Drake Sutton for destroying her ability to do both.

Suddenly furious at all the man had cost her, she picked up the phone and dialed a taxi service. Ten minutes later, the cabdriver pulled up to Sutton's estate. Nerves tingled in Stella's stomach. Sutton, Kat and Jaycee had probably meant to kill her at Luke's cabin. If she went in now, they might finish the job.

But she couldn't bow to the fear. She had to confront Sutton, force him to admit the truth about her mother and those other children.

She spoke into the security intercom, identifying herself and asking for Sutton. The doors slid open, and the driver sped up the long narrow driveway, then deposited her at the entrance. She paid the driver with some bills Luke had left on the dresser, and climbed out. Sucking in a sharp breath, she started to press the doorbell, but the butler opened the door before she could do so, and ushered her to Drake Sutton's study.

He was perched behind his desk with a pipe lit in his hand, looking austere and angry.

"You tried to kill me, didn't you?" she said without preamble.

He chuckled wryly. "Not I, Stella. But there are some who don't trust you."

She arched a brow. "And you do?"

"You always return to me in the end." He gestured for her to sit, but she declined.

"I came for answers."

He sighed. "I thought we covered the past a few days ago when I bailed you out of jail."

"Not everything," Stella said. "I want the truth about my mother. About how I came to live with you."

"You have had memories?" he asked gruffly.

"Some. I remember crying for her at night. Wondering if she'd come back, if you had her locked in another room."

"Don't be ridiculous."

"Why is that ridiculous? I know you brainwashed me, tortured me, gave me shock treatments."

His gaze cut away from her, toward the fireplace. "You were a hard one to break. My finest piece of work, though."

"I was not an object," Stella said, furious. "I was a little girl!"

He turned back to her, his expression lethal. "I gave you a home, a place to live and cared for you when your mother didn't want you."

"You're saying she gave me up? I thought my parents died in an accident."

He hesitated. "I never wanted you to know the truth."

He rose, circled around the desk and faced her. "You see I'm not the monster you believe me to be. I saved you and protected you."

"You stole me from my mother, you probably killed her—"

"No, Stella. You want the truth?" His voice rose an octave. "I didn't steal you, your mother sold you."

Stella gasped and staggered backward, grasping the chair for support. "No…"

"Yes, Stella. The other children in the dorm were orphans. But your mother wanted money so she offered you up."

Anguish robbed Stella's breath. "And you bought me?"

"I stepped in to protect you."

"And why would you do that?" Stella asked. "Why did you save me from the fire and not the others?"

Sutton reached out to touch her, but Stella stiffened and backed away. "Tell me. Did you think I'd make a better killer?"

He shook his head. "No, Stella, I saved you because you are my daughter."

Stella collapsed into the chair. No. She couldn't be this ruthless man's child.

It meant she'd be tied to him forever.

Chapter Eleven

Luke's mind boomeranged between trusting Stella and asking another agent with objectivity to replace him.

But he had to see Stella first. Follow his instincts. See if she'd slip up.

Hell, he wanted to see her anyway, just to confirm that she was safe.

But he had to remain objective.

His cell phone rang, and he glanced at the caller ID screen. His superior, Spencer. He grunted a curse, and answered. "Devlin."

"You haven't checked in, Devlin. What's going on?"

Luke relayed his conversation with Hall, Quinn Salt, and his findings about the project.

"So you think Stella Segall was one of these children? How convenient."

"She has memories of being sensory deprived, of undergoing shock therapy. She appears to be suffering from Post Traumatic Syndrome."

"Or she's faking it," Spencer shot back. "Where is she now?"

"I left her at the safe house alone."

"And you trust her?" Spencer cursed.

Luke grimaced. "Yes."

"You're a damn fool, Devlin," Spencer snapped. "Maybe Sutton told her about this project, and she's fabricating these nightmares to gain your sympathy. First she seduces you, then she returns and entices you to buy into some sob story. When are you going to realize that her behavior is purely devious?"

Luke refused to admit verbally Spencer might be right.

But the bigger question that plagued him was if Stella's treatment could be reversed. He'd have to discuss the matter with the FBI psychologist.

Deprogramming would be her only defense if the worst happened. After all, the prognosis for battered and severely abused children was dismal. Many victims turned out to be serial killers, rapists, sociopaths, suicidal at best. As Quinn had stated, very few ever lived a normal life.

The episode at the river where Stella had almost drowned rose to haunt him.

"I'll keep you posted," Luke said, then hung up before Spencer could argue. The man was an icon at the bureau. Luke's erratic actions the past year had lost him credibility. But he still had to rely on his instincts. If a man lost that on the job, he had nothing.

And he was walking the ledge…had been for some time.

He neared the safe house and was surprised that most of the lights were off. Maybe Stella had crawled into bed to rest.

The image taunted him to forget his mission and join her, but he hardened his resolve as he parked and scanned the property in case someone had located them. When he entered the house, the lights were off, and silence engulfed him, sending a bad vibe down his spine. Either she was asleep or she wasn't inside.

His pulse accelerated as he checked the den and found it empty. He tiptoed to the guest bedroom and peeked inside. The bed was still made, the curtains drawn. No Stella.

He gritted his teeth, his gut reaction one of fear that someone had gotten to Stella. But so far, nothing looked disturbed.

His next thought was that she had left of her own accord. Which meant that she might have returned to Sutton's.

And be working against Luke.

Lying to him. Making a fool out of his impossible attraction to her.

Unnerved by both possibilities, he quickly checked the other bedroom but found it undisturbed as well.

Frustrated, he stalked back to the living room area. Then he spotted a notepad on the end table. The top sheet of paper had been torn away, but an indention on the following sheet resembled letters. He grabbed a pencil, placed it on its side and rubbed back and forth until the words below appeared.

The number for a cab company.

Damn.

He phoned the cab company, identified himself, then threatened to report the man who answered for interfering with an investigation of a possible kidnapping if he didn't cooperate. Wavering, the man checked his dispatch person, then connected Luke to the cabdriver.

"I'm looking for information. It's urgent." Luke recited the address of the safe house, gave Stella's description, then asked for the address where the man had dropped her.

The street name the driver reported back matched Drake Sutton's.

"Did she look upset? Under duress?" Luke asked.

"A little nervous maybe. She kept fidgeting with the door handle, but there was no one else in the cab. No one put a gun to her head."

Luke thanked him then hung up, the realization that Stella might still be working with Sutton staring him boldly in the face.

A fraction of a second later, the sound of an engine roared outside. He checked his weapon, then peered out of the corner of the window. A cab stopped in front of the house. He held his breath as Stella climbed from the taxi and walked up the driveway.

Another car appeared on its tail. A dark sedan.

Suddenly gunfire blasted through the air. The cab screeched away. Stella screamed and ran toward the house. He opened the door, dove behind the porch column, then fired into the darkness. Stella threw herself to the ground, then crawled through the grass toward him while he tried to cover her.

The bullets continued flying, pinging right at her.

STELLA CLUTCHED at the ground, dodging the bullets, but one nicked her shoulder, and she dropped even lower onto the grass, throwing her hands over her head for protection. Luke fired rapid shots in succession, yelling at her to stay down. Sutton's warning that she had to help him or Luke would die echoed in her head, but the shooter wasn't Sutton. Her father.

No, she'd never call him that.

She belly-crawled her way to the porch just as the car sped away. Luke jumped off the porch and kept firing, grabbing her by the arm. She winced but jumped up and clung to him as they ran inside the house.

As soon as they were safe, he swung her around, anger and concern darkening his eyes. "Are you all right?" He moved toward her to check her wound, but she waved him off.

"I'm fine. I just got grazed."

"Let me look at it."

"No, Luke, I'll clean it up later."

He gave her a blistering stare. "Who the hell was that, and where have you been?"

She held up a hand to calm him. "Luke, I can explain."

"The hell you can. You led the damn perps right to the safe house." He grabbed his cell phone and motioned her to the door. "Come on. I'll find us another location. Then I expect you to talk."

She swallowed the knot of fear in her chest. She'd almost died out there and wanted nothing more than for Luke to hold her. Make her forget that she was Sutton's daughter, and that her mother had sold her to be turned into a killer.

But she'd endangered Luke when she'd intended to protect him by playing along with Sutton.

Luke hustled her toward the car, and she hunched inside, rubbing her arm where her shoulder throbbed. Blood seeped through her shirt, but she didn't complain. She deserved what she'd gotten. She just didn't know how to make things right.

"This is Devlin," he said into the phone. "We need another safe house." He hesitated, and she assumed he was talking to Detective Black.

Stella wondered if Sutton had tapped Luke's line. His earlier threat had proven his desperation to keep her under his thumb. Sutton would kill anyone she cared about if it meant keeping her in line. She should have been more careful. Should have noticed someone following her...

Luke accelerated, and they raced from the island to a smaller one called Lady's Isle. A few tense minutes later, he parked in back of a beach cottage that looked ancient but would do for the night.

"Black's sending over another car to swap with us."

She nodded, and followed him. Her stomach churned when they stepped inside the den. He flipped on the overhead light, led her to the bathroom and began to pull at her shirt. "You're hit. Let me see your wound. Then we'll talk."

She grabbed his hands. "Luke stop, let me explain."

His eyes met hers in the mirror, the coldness back. "Tell me why, Stella. Why did you go back to Sutton? Because you're using me? Working against me? Has everything between us been a lie?"

She didn't ask how he knew she'd been with Sutton. He was an FBI agent. He had his ways. Just as Sutton did.

"No, it's not like that, Luke."

Luke reached for her shirt again, but Stella pushed his hands away. Guilt ate at her. She couldn't accept his help.

Yet she wanted him desperately at the same time.

"I can clean the wound." She peeled the blouse off her shoulder to expose the bloody flesh. The bullet had grazed the skin, but wasn't embedded. She reached for a washcloth to dampen it, but Luke did it instead. His breath bathed her neck as he gently blotted the blood from her wound.

"Does it hurt?" he asked gruffly.

"It's fine." Tears stung her eyes at his kindness.

"Then why do you look like you're going to cry?"

Sutton's intimidation tactics flashed back. "Let's just say I didn't hear the answers from Sutton that I'd wanted."

His hand stilled, then the other gently massaged her arm. She glanced in the mirror and saw him watching her over her shoulder.

His cold look softened. "What did you learn, Stella?"

That Sutton is my father.

No, she couldn't admit to that. It was too shameful. "I…asked him about my mother. How I came to stay with him."

"And?"

"When I was growing up, he told me that she'd been in a boating accident. The other day he said she'd abandoned me. But today he admitted that…that she sold me instead."

The barest of a reaction flashed in Luke's gaze. Disbelief. Disgust. Pity.

"She sold you for money?"

"Apparently so. According to Sutton, he saved me."

Luke muttered a curse. "Saved you from what?"

"I...don't know. He allowed them to use me in their sick experiments." She hesitated, wondering if it would have been better if he'd let her die in the fire.

"He lied before, Stella. Who's to say he isn't lying now?"

Stella shrugged. She didn't know what to believe anymore. "There's something else," Stella said, her pain spilling over in her voice. "Today, when you were at the fire...I had flashbacks of the blaze that destroyed the orphanage. I remembered some of the other children."

"And?"

He traced a finger along her cheek, brushing her hair away. The movement was both erotic and so tender that an ache settled in her chest.

If she'd once been a hardened agent or killer, she certainly had fallen from the role.

"They died," she said quietly. Her chest shook with unshed emotions. "I...remember hearing them scream, begging Sutton to go back and save them, but it was too late. They died in the fire."

Luke dropped his head forward, then pulled her back against him and slid his arms around her. "God, Stella."

The dam of emotions burst, and her tears overflowed. Heart-wrenching sobs racked her body, the memories and horrors flooding back. "There was another man there, too, Luke, someone they called the Master."

"The Master? What did he do?"

"He administered the treatments. He was a monster."

Luke pressed her head into his shoulder and stroked her back. "Shh, it's all right."

"No, I should have died, too, Luke. Don't you see? Sutton saved me instead of the other girls, then turned me into a freak. A killer."

Luke rocked her back and forth, then slowly led her to the bedroom and pulled her down beside him. Stella fell into his embrace, her heart breaking for the other kids who had lost their lives.

And for the innocence she'd lost as well.

She'd never forgive Sutton for what he'd done to her and those other children.

And she'd never, ever call him her father. A father didn't turn his own daughter into a killer.

LUKE PRESSED tender kisses to Stella's head, massaging her back and shoulders as she spent her emotions. His own heart ached for her. She had endured so much, and he sensed she'd never been shown any tenderness or real love.

Damn Drake Sutton.

He would make sure the bastard paid.

But Sutton obviously hadn't been working alone. Luke had to find his conspirators and see that they were punished as well. And this man—the Master. He wanted to torture him the way he had Stella.

Stella's tears finally subsided, and she curled into him, her hand gently stroking his chest. He threaded his fingers through her hair, wound the ebony strands around his fingers, felt such intense hunger and protective feelings that he wished they could lie there forever. Secure together, away from the rest of the world and its horrors.

Stella slid a hand up and caressed his cheek with her

fingers, and his body hardened. Her tear-misted eyes searched his, begging, hoping, yearning. Knowing he was still walking a tightrope but unable to stop himself, he lowered his head and claimed her mouth. Her lips were soft, supple, her tiny moan of acquiesce nearly his undoing. He deepened the kiss, tasting her innocence, her pain, her need in the way she clung to him. She cupped his face and dropped delicate kisses along his jaw, his ear, then his neck. He spread his hands along her back and drew her tighter, savoring the way her body fit with his, the way she plucked at heartstrings he hadn't known existed.

He'd vowed not to make love to her until she could give herself to him completely.

He didn't know what was happening to him here, but he wasn't a hundred percent sure he could keep his promise.

Yes, he could. But he could still give her pleasure. Prove he wasn't a selfish madman like Sutton.

Her kisses grew more passionate, the touches more urgent. His heart racing, he lowered his head, tasted the flesh of her neck, then swept her shirt away and teased her nipples through the flimsy lace bra. The stiff peaks begged for more, and he gave them his rapt attention, stripping the lingerie until he clenched the rigid peak of her nipple between his teeth. The weight of her other breast spilled over his palm, and he kneaded it while drinking in the blissful titillation of the other. She slid her leg between his, stroking his calf with her foot.

"I need you, Luke."

Her softly murmured plea drove him crazy. He suckled her other breast until she bucked and scraped her nails across his back, urging him to take more, to give her pleasure. He walked her backward to the bedroom and lowered them to the bed. Then he flipped her over, stripped her warm-ups and underwear, and removed his own clothes. Finally he crawled on top of her. He started at her neck, then licked and sucked his way down her shoulders, to her spine, the arch of her back, her buttocks.

She groaned and protested, tried to reverse positions, but he held her prisoner to his teasing just as he was a prisoner to her desires. His hard length pressed against her, and he pushed her legs apart, fitting his shaft between them, teasing, stroking, rubbing her until she cried out into the pillow.

"Please, Luke, please, I want you."

She clutched the sheets with her nails as he rolled her over to face him, then pushed her legs apart and positioned them over his shoulders. His own body hardened as he dipped lower to find her center with his tongue. She was already wet from wanting him, her body spasming with her orgasm. He tasted the heart of her, lapped and loved her precious body until she trembled and quivered from her release.

"Luke, please..."

He rose above her with shaky arms, cradled her face in his hands. "I made you a promise."

"Don't stop now," she cried. "I may be broken, but take me as I am, Luke. I need you."

He looked into her eyes and wondered if she were right. If she really was broken. If so, maybe his loving could mend her.

Take me as I am.

The anguish and hunger in her eyes was such a heady combination that he couldn't deny her. She wet her lips, slid her hand over his erection and began to stroke him, slowly rubbing from the base of his hard length to the tip. He pulsed and throbbed in her hand, knowing he wouldn't release himself this way. If he came, they'd do it together. Him inside her. Her quivering around him.

She flicked a tongue across his nipple and swirled her finger across his sex again, tempting him. Her pleading eyes sent him over the edge. They were the eyes of a woman who'd never been loved.

That was the gift he could give her.

Hating himself for not being strong enough to keep his promise, but unable to deny them any longer, he grabbed a condom from his pants, then rolled it on. When he looked down, she was watching. Staring. Smiling.

Her seduction was dangerous.

But complete, as he slid himself inside her.

One moment of blissful, slow teasing, and she grabbed his buttocks and begged him to pump harder. He did. Thrusting deeper and deeper each time, increasing the rhythm until they were both sweating and aching.

"Oh, Luke…."

Her husky words ignited the fire in his loins to a fever pitch, and he lifted her rear, angling her so he could sink himself to her core. When he pushed to her depths, she reached for his hands, clung to them as he thrust into her again and again. The first spasms of her orgasm flowed around him as his own willpower splintered, and relief spilled through him.

When he glanced into her heady gaze, he knew that he'd crossed the line once again. This time, he'd not only made love to her, but he'd lost his soul as well.

He only prayed it was worth it....

Chapter Twelve

Luke hugged Stella to him, inhaling the sweet fragrance of her raspberry shampoo as he savored the last remnants of the morning. Stella sighed and curled into him, mumbling his name as he stroked her hair.

What had happened to the hardened agent who never crossed the line? Now all the lines intersected, curved and darted off in tangents so he didn't know which direction to travel.

Move forward with a personal relationship with Stella?

How could he when he didn't know the truth about her or her feelings toward him?

Her hair brushed his cheek, offering a view of the small scar behind her ear again, and his stomach knotted. She couldn't help it that she'd been victimized as a child.

Yet had she really turned the corner?

Stella rolled away from him, fighting with the covers. "Kill…Devlin. Yes, Master."

He froze, stiffening by her side as she whispered the words again.

"Yes. Kill Devlin."

He eased his arm from behind her and sat up. Dammit. He'd begun to trust her when she obviously hadn't outrun her nightmares. And how did he know for sure that she hadn't been programmed or trained to seduce him again, then strike when he was least expecting it? Maybe she'd been given a hypnotic suggestion that could be triggered by a phone call or a word or a symbol.

Had he once again been sleeping with the enemy?

"Luke?"

He squared his shoulders and stood, facing the bed. Her eyes slid over him, seductive, sultry, asking for a repeat performance of the night before.

Asking for more than he could give.

Because if he took her again this morning, he'd be lost all over again.

And he had a job to do. Find a monster who'd tortured young children, stolen their identity and childhood and turned them into soldiers.

"I need to get on the case, and meet my contact."

Disappointment flared momentarily in her eyes. "Can I come with you?"

"No." He couldn't take a chance, not and break Quinn's cover.

She raised up on her knees, her breasts swaying as she traced a finger down his bare chest. His sex surged and rose toward her. She smiled, cupped his face in her hands and kissed him. A slow, sultry kiss meant to entice him to return to bed.

God help him, it almost worked.

But the memory of her calling his name in passion, then talking about killing him in her sleep, stopped him cold.

"Last night was so wonderful, Luke. What's wrong now?"

He chewed the inside of his cheek. "You were repeating commands in your sleep, Stella. Commands to kill me."

THE EUPHORIA of the night before slowly seeped from Stella's body. Luke's erection, which had been begging for her a moment earlier, vanished as well.

"I said that?"

He nodded, and she wrapped the covers around her, the urge to hide setting in. Doubts about herself followed.

"I must have been having another nightmare."

"Probably."

Distrust lingered between them, though, tainting their lovemaking and the warm cocoon that had enveloped them as they'd slept. She craved Luke's arms around her again, wanted him murmuring soft tender nothings, doing wicked things to her body.

But she had no right to ask such a thing. She certainly couldn't expect it.

His gaze locked with hers, questions, doubt, uncertainty lingering between them. Unable to make him promises she couldn't keep, she watched him walk to the shower, aching to join him. Finally resigned, she stood, wrapped the sheet around her and studied herself in the mirror. Curious about the tattoo mark, she found a small mirror in the dresser and angled it so she could see the back of her ear. The symbol Luke had noticed.

Sutton had branded her, made her a number, not a

person. She wanted to scrub away the tattoo, but it had been permanently etched into her skin as if it marked her for life. And it signified that Sutton had controlled her, body, soul and mind.

The only way she could ever be free and love Luke completely was to rid herself of this unwanted connection between her and Sutton.

Unbidden, the truth came to her—the only way to do that was to kill him.

She closed her eyes, imagined herself loading a gun. The act seemed natural. More disturbing images flashed into her head—images of target shooting when she was young. Of staring at cardboard signs that resembled humans and firing. Images of training exercises with blanks where the kids formed teams, were dropped into deserted areas, forced to survive for weeks on end, taught to take on the enemy with no hesitation.

She saw a body falling, a stranger, and wondered if he were real or if he'd been a hologram—another method they used for simulation battles.

The shower water clicked off, jerking her from her memories, and she dropped her hands to her sides. She hadn't realized she'd raised them, had mimicked holding the gun until she saw her steadfast reflection in the mirror.

Could she kill Sutton if it meant escaping him?

He had rescued her from the fire when she was a child. Acted as a substitute father when her mother had sold her. Claimed he was her blood father.

Yet, how could he say he loved her?

He couldn't, not and order her to kill the only person in the world she actually cared about. The only one who might be able to save her wicked, lost soul…

"LOOK, KAT, JAYCEE, I have Stella under control." Sutton gestured for them to seat themselves in the office so he could explain. "I know you two tried to kill her when she went to Devlin."

"We were following orders," Kat said matter-of-factly.

"She's been a ticking bomb for the past fifteen months," Jaycee added. "Ever since she met Luke Devlin."

"I told you she wasn't up for the assignment." Kat stretched her long, lithe legs in front of her. "You should have let me at him."

"Or me," Jaycee murmured with a sly grin.

Sutton arched a brow, his voice low but lethal. "Don't tell me you two are attracted to that damn agent, too? What is it with the man?"

Kat grinned, one hand trailing over tight, black leather pants. "He has a commanding presence," she admitted. "And I would have enjoyed taunting him before killing him."

"Yes," Jaycee said in a low voice. "It would have been fun to watch him beg for mercy."

Sutton almost grinned. The experiment had worked so much better with Kat and Jaycee. Maybe he had been too soft with Stella.

"What's done is done," Sutton said. "But rest assured, I found a way to manipulate Stella."

Kat and Jaycee exchanged worried looks. "How?" Jaycee asked.

"If she doesn't help us, Devlin is dead."

Both women nodded. "Just say the word," Jaycee said.

"We'll eliminate both of them together," Kat added.

Sutton swallowed. Kat and Jaycee would follow through and have no regrets afterward. "Now, what have you found out about the work at Nighthawk Island?"

Kat leaned forward, practically purring. "We think there's an undercover agent there now. I'm working on unearthing his identity."

Sutton swallowed. Maybe they could turn the agent and use him to their advantage.

But he wanted names of projects. Results. Something he could sell to the highest bidder.

Some way to redeem himself to the Master for this mess with Stella. The Master had taught him not to let things get personal. And he had failed. Meaning he was disposable.

LUKE HAD TO PUT some distance between himself and Stella. Focus on the case. Find out who was behind Sutton and obtain evidence on the details of the experiment years ago. It was the only way he could nail Sutton and free Stella from his evil grasp.

After that, Luke had no idea what would happen between them.

But he could probably cut a deal for the handler's shooting in exchange for her testimony against Sutton. Afterward, he might be able to arrange a therapist who could counteract the brainwashing she'd suffered.

Knowing that if he joined Stella in the shower and

saw her naked again, he'd make love to her, he left while the water was still running. En route to the police headquarters, he made a quick phone call to his superior.

"What's going on?" Spencer asked.

"Just checking in," Luke answered.

"Do you have Stella Segall under watch?"

"I've moved her to another safe house."

"Then you left her alone again?"

Luke hesitated. "Yes."

"Devlin, she's not the victimized woman she appears to be on the surface. I didn't want to tell you this, but I have photos of her and J.T. Osborne together."

Luke's stomach plummeted. "What?"

"I told you Osborne wasn't trustworthy. He was helping Stella and Sutton."

Luke swallowed hard in denial. No... He'd trusted J.T. Trusted Stella.

"You're saying they were involved?"

"They were sleeping together, yes."

Luke's lungs tightened as pain and betrayal knifed through him. He'd defended J.T. Had sent his wife and son money. Had put his career on the line insisting J.T. was not corrupt.

Myra's words rose to taunt him. "I think J.T.'s seeing another woman."

Luke had reassured her that J.T. wasn't a cheater. And if J.T. had slipped, Luke would have never considered he'd slept with Stella. J.T. had never even mentioned that he knew her.

She met you right after J.T.'s death. Maybe the meeting wasn't a coincidence....

God, he felt like a fool.

And J.T.'s death—Luke had suspected murder. Could Stella be responsible?

"Devlin?" Spencer snapped. "Give me the address of the safe house, and I'll assign a tail to Stella."

Sweat trickled down Luke's neck. He felt sick to his stomach. "Yeah. Okay." Luke recited the address, wondering how he could have been so stupid.

"Don't blow Quinn's cover at CIRP," Spencer muttered.

Luke frowned and pulled into the precinct. "Don't worry. I'll take care of this myself. It's too risky having him poke around for me on Nighthawk Island."

"What are you looking for exactly?" Spencer asked.

"Sutton had a conspirator years ago," Luke answered. "I think that person is still pulling the strings."

A long pause followed. "Just keep me posted."

Luke agreed and hung up. Five minutes later, he gulped down a cup of coffee, desperately trying to banish the J.T.-Stella scenario from his head, while Black filled him in on everything he'd learned about Nighthawk Island.

"Here's a basic sketch of the island." Black pointed to several buildings on a map. "This is the main hub of the research park. There are also a few smaller buildings located on the other side of the island with decontamination units."

All in all, the island was a few miles across. But Luke would have to go in on foot to avoid security. Then it would take time to make the trek to the main facility.

"Security cameras are scattered at various points around the research park." Black marked them on the map, then pointed to a cove about four miles down from CIRP's main headquarters. "This is the best entry point. Because of the cliffs and lack of security, you can sneak a small fishing boat in, hide it in the cove for escape, then lose yourself in these woods until you weave your way up to the facility."

Then would come the difficult part. Sneaking inside. Gaining access to password-protected computer files.

Luke thanked him, then left. Armed with water and ammunition, he phoned Quinn to ask for assistance. Quinn directed him to a south entrance where he would deactivate the security long enough for Luke to enter. After that, he'd be on his own.

It took Luke another half an hour to arrange a fishing boat at the marina, then he rowed his way toward the island, careful to follow Black's instructions so he wouldn't be spotted in his approach. Stella's image kept popping into his head during the trek, the tension mounting within him. He had never felt this way about a woman before.

Never saw a possible traitor as a victim. Never considered his own partner might betray him, or that Stella's deception had cut so deep.

Never wanted so hard to deny the obvious truth.

Luke scrubbed his hand over his neck in frustration, fighting the urge to justify Stella's actions, to clear her.

The waves rocked the boat back and forth, the force of the tide trying to sweep him in the opposite direction. He had to focus to stay on track. Saltwater stung his face, the misty spray cooling his sweating body. Finally he maneuvered the boat into the cove, tied it to a rock jutting from the bank, and began the hike to the Nighthawk Island facility.

STELLA STARED at the empty bed where she and Luke had made love, a desolate feeling overwhelming her. Would her life always be like this? Her mind scattered with terrible, sporadic memories? Her nights filled with wanting and yearning for Luke, yet knowing that one day he'd desert her in the end just as he had this morning?

With her unable to confess her feelings for him, that she loved him?

Her heart swelled as emotions crowded in, fighting for space with the tumultuous feelings pouring through her. Feelings of abandonment. Of being used and abused. Of being thrown away by her mother, then sheltered by a monster who claimed to be her father?

Luke deserved so much better. He was a man of his word. A man who fought for justice. A man who had jeopardized his career for her.

How could she repay him?

"I don't want you to pay me back," he had muttered.

But she knew no other way to show him how she felt than to do just that.

Killing Sutton was one way. Finding out the details of his organization so she could pass them on to Luke and shut down Sutton's operations, another.

Determined, she dressed in a pair of jeans and a black T-shirt she found in the closet, although she had to roll up the pants slightly. Then she phoned the cab service she'd used the day before. On the off chance, Sutton or his security guards would see the cab and discover the location of the safe house, she instructed the driver to drop her a couple of blocks from Sutton's estate. She walked the rest of the way, this time buzzing the security at the gate, and entering with the hopes of convincing Sutton she had willingly converted to his side.

That she was using Luke.

The butler escorted her in and ushered her to Sutton's study. He appeared a moment later, a smug look on his face. "So, you've decided to accept my deal?"

"I don't really have a choice, do I? You've always had control."

He smiled as if he'd accepted her acquiescence, which only angered her more.

"What exactly do you want from me, Drake?"

"What kind of information does Devlin have about me? Who does he have on the inside at Nighthawk Island?"

"I don't know the answer to that."

"Come on, Stella. No pillow talk last night?"

Not the way he'd meant. "No. He doesn't exactly trust me now."

"And you trust him, darling?" He unwrapped a cigar and sniffed it. "You don't think he's romancing you to get information on us?"

A sliver of doubt wormed its way into Stella. Of course, that was possible.

But the memory of Luke making love to her returned, the husky way he'd murmured that he wanted her completely. He had meant that statement, hadn't he?

Or was she so starved for love that she'd fallen for a lie?

It didn't matter. Even if she had no place to turn when she finished, she wanted away from Sutton and the life he'd created for her.

"I don't trust anyone," Stella said. "And I want to review information on all of my assignments."

Sutton studied her for a long moment, then nodded and buzzed his office downstairs. "Kat, Stella's on her way down. Give her complete access to the data on her missions."

Stella thanked him, then headed to the basement office to face her old life.

LUKE DUCKED between the tall trees, grateful he had studied the layout of the island beforehand, and hoping that the security system hadn't been expanded since Detective Black's last analysis. Twice he thought he might have detected motion sensors, but decided the sunshine slanting through the layers of leaves had sparked his attention. He half wished he'd waited until night so the darkness could camouflage his appearance, but forged ahead, deciding a daytime visit would trigger less suspicion than a nighttime one.

The sound of a bird squawking made him pause, reminding him of the unique nighthawk that inhabited the island. The unusual bird of prey had been known to attack man as well as animal.

Had the bird been the result of some kind of crossbreeding experiment, or genetic engineering?

Or maybe the scientists tortured animals as part of their research in prelude to trial studies on people.

A half hour later, he located the lab coat Quinn had left for him in a pile of brush, slipped it on, then veered around to the side door where Quinn was supposed to meet him. Luke had seen a photo of the facility from Black's files, and heard sinister stories about the place, although from the outside, it resembled any other research hospital facility. Cold. Sterile. A place where modern science could work miracles through new technology. A place where some strove to save lives, constantly upgrade medical treatments and cure diseases.

A place where ethics were also challenged. Where some died or were murdered to protect the secrets inside.

Quinn must have been watching through a window, because he met Luke at the door and ushered him in. They walked down the hall, through a secured area where Quinn used his security card to gain entrance, then Luke followed Quinn to a small office. He closed the door as soon as they were inside.

"I've reset the security cameras, so you have approximately thirty minutes to get in and out without detection. All of the old files, any research conducted through CIRP and the prior facility and hospital here, can be located in this database." He punched in his access code, then turned the system over to Luke.

"Thanks, Quinn. Now get out of here."

Quinn gave him a worried look. "Are you sure? If someone finds you here—"

"I won't jeopardize your cover, not after what happened to J.T. If I get caught, I'll handle it." Luke hardened his voice. "Understood? No racing in to save me. Your role here is more important. Besides, Spencer knows I'm here. If anything happens, he'll cover me."

Quinn hesitated, but nodded, then left Luke to study the files. Luke's anger over the project involving Stella intensified as he read the data.

The project originated during the Cold War, and had been called SHIP—an acronym signifying the creation of the perfect secret agent, one who possessed superhuman intelligence and power, but who possessed no emotion. A group of children, who were genetically enhanced as babies were either raised in total isolation or in small groups, and trained at an early age through brainwashing techniques. The genetic therapy supposedly focused on increasing their physical strength, cognitive abilities, fine motor skills and agility and attempted to decrease, and if possible, completely eradicate emotional responses.

Another group was used as a comparative study. These were normal children who'd been orphaned.

His chest tightened. Stella had been one of those.

So her memories were very real.

He read further, notes on the experiments and torture techniques sickening him. He'd seen depraved acts committed against children before, but still didn't understand how someone could do such awful things to them, especially in such a coldhearted manner. The children hadn't been treated as humans at all, but as subjects.

He scrubbed a hand through his hair and sighed in disgust, but forced himself to continue.

An explosion in the facility had set the building on fire. Sutton had rushed in to save the kids, and rescued Stella. Most of the others had died, and Sutton had taken Stella to live with him. The project had been deemed a failure because the orphans' emotional responses couldn't be erased. Also, the more often the first group was placed in social situations, the more they developed a human side—a side with a conscience that rendered them imperfect. Definitely not the success the experimental team had hoped for.

The explosion and subsequent fire at the center garnered government attention and bad publicity. That, coupled with the lack of funding, the need for more extensive genetic work and the end of the Cold War, forced the scientists to disband the project.

Luke grimaced. Sutton had obviously not given up. He'd kept Stella isolated and bound to him, and continued the project on his own. Kat and Jaycee had also been subjects. He'd brainwashed the girls into believing he was their savior, yet he'd destroyed their lives and free will instead.

Luke folded his hands into fists, his anger mounting. He wanted to rip off Sutton's head and tear his body apart, limb by limb. Torture him the way Sutton had Stella and those other children.

But Sutton wasn't working alone. And Luke had to find his partner in crime.

Even then, could he forget that Stella had been with J.T.? And what would he tell J.T.'s wife?

Voices sounded outside, and he rushed to copy the file, but suddenly the door opened and two guards stormed in, their weapons drawn.

Luke slid one hand down to reach for his gun, but the men aimed automatics his way. One guard pointed his weapon at Luke's head while the other targeted his hand, following Luke's movement.

A second later, the sound of a man's deep voice filled the room. "Put down your weapon, Agent Devlin. There is no escape."

Chapter Thirteen

Stella read the files, flashes of memories resurfacing that she didn't want to face. She'd stolen notes on biological warfare experiments and given them to a man named Iska Milaski, a known terrorist who only a few weeks ago had been connected to a rash of suicides in Savannah. The suicides had eventually turned out to be murders via a deadly virus the victims had contracted through Milaski's doing. The man was supposed to be dead, but his body hadn't been recovered.

Another agent, Mark Steele, had helped Luke solve the case. Before that, Luke had lost a partner, a man named J.T. Osborne. For some reason, the name teased her memory banks, but Stella couldn't pinpoint why. The FBI suspected Osborne's death was related to Nighthawk Island but, as yet, had no proof.

She froze momentarily, fear knifing through her. Snippets of conversations echoed through her head. The day she'd met Luke, he'd mentioned that he'd recently lost a partner.

But she'd already known that.

Her chest clenched. She had met Osborne. She saw his face in her mind. Heard his voice in her head.

Dear God. She hadn't killed Luke's partner, had she?

Shaken by the thought, she read further. Two years ago, she'd seduced a scientist in Germany into her confidence and had robbed him of confidential information regarding a new treatment for brain tumors. Another case that disturbed her even more went back five years—apparently she'd worked with Kat and Jaycee on the assassination of a U.S. government official who had discovered that Sutton's original project from the Cold War was still alive.

The original project had centered around her, Kat and Jaycee.

"Is the past coming back to you now?" Kat asked.

Stella stared into the woman's insidious eyes, and nodded. "Bits and pieces."

She turned to address Jaycee along with Kat. "Did you know that we were all part of a research experiment? That Sutton and his people brainwashed us to be agents and killers when we were children?"

Kat shrugged. "We are what we are."

"You question things too much," Jaycee agreed. "Sutton is our family. We owe him."

Did they?

If he'd cared about them, why would he have used them for vile purposes?

"Are there other survivors, kids programed like us to be agents?" Stella asked.

Kat shook her head. "Not that we're aware of. I think the rest of them died in the fire."

Nadine's and Bianca's small faces flashed into Stella's mind, making her chest ache.

But warning bells clanged in her head. Betraying

Sutton meant sudden death for her. She faintly remembered having that discussion with Raul, but he'd assured her he would help her escape.

She gripped the counter, realizing that she'd just discovered another piece of the puzzle. Raul had been trying to help her leave Sutton, not threatening to expose her.

So why would she have killed him?

"If you don't cooperate with Sutton now, he'll eliminate Devlin himself," Kat said.

Stella jerked back to the reality of her situation. The only way for Luke to survive was for her to keep her bargain with Sutton. To use Luke.

But how would she ever be able to pull it off? How could she betray him again or forget him? She couldn't. Her heart burned just thinking about never seeing Luke again. Of never lying in his arms or making love to him.

The only way to rid herself of wanting Luke was to let Sutton erase her memories of Luke.

But that would mean truly relinquishing her control again and submitting totally to Sutton's commands…

LUKE LOST CONSCIOUSNESS for the half-dozenth time. So far, the guards had locked him in a small, dark room, beaten him senseless, and threatened his life—all because they wanted him to disclose the name of the federal agent on the inside at Nighthawk Island.

Luke hadn't been able to save J.T. He sure as hell wouldn't reveal Quinn's identity. He'd rather die himself.

A six-foot-five man made of steel they called the Tank gave the orders. His voice had echoed over the intercom in the lab, and he had continued to watch as the guards had beaten Luke. Luke's head throbbed, his left arm had been twisted so hard it had nearly been wrenched from the socket, and he'd coughed up blood for half an hour. Pain rippled through his chest as if he'd sustained several broken ribs.

One of the guards jammed a gun against his temple. "We want answers, Devlin."

"I told you, we don't have anyone undercover here at the moment. If we did, don't you think they'd be here now, trying to help me escape?"

The other guard rammed his fist into Luke's stomach, then laughed as Luke nearly choked on the blood. "Then how the hell did you get into that secured area?"

"I'm a whiz kid at breaking codes." Luke shot him an icy glare. "That's why they brought me into the FBI."

"Right," the man muttered sarcastically. Another fist in his belly, and Luke had to inhale to prevent himself from passing out.

"Now, tell me," he said, angling his head toward Tank, "why you're determined to hide a project that was conducted over twenty years ago?"

The man laughed. "You know the answer to that, Devlin."

"Because the project never died?" His stomach heaved at the thought that there might be another set of children being tortured.

The Tank shrugged. "Genetic enhancement is the wave of the future. Wouldn't you rather raise and train a special elite group of isolated subjects as soldiers than draft innocent young men and women with families to do the nasty work for us?"

"Torturing children is not the answer."

"We don't care what you think. You are dispensable."

"Then why not just shoot me and get it over with?"

"Because we want a name." He shrugged nonchalantly, dark hair falling over one eye. "I'm growing tired of your lack of response. You have exactly ten minutes to think it through."

"I won't change my mind."

"You won't have to. We're preparing a dose of our truth serum." He ground his face into Luke's, sinister eyes meeting his with a calculating look that only a cold-blooded killer could possess. "Like it or not, you will tell us the truth before you die. And it won't be an easy death." He ran the tip of his gun over Luke's torso. "You see, our truth serum has its own unique blend. It paralyzes the limbs and muscles, even the eyelids, while the rest of the body implodes on itself." He chuckled. "There is so much pain, yet you can barely even make your vocal chords work to scream."

Both the guards and the Tank left the room at the same time, filing out like soldiers. Luke gritted his teeth, glanced around for an escape route, then began to unravel the ropes that held his hands tied behind his back.

His ribs felt as if knives pierced his chest as he twisted and worked at the knots. A dizzy spell engulfed him, blood trickling from his jaw and lip. He blinked to focus and stay conscious, struggling to hurry. Finally he loosened the knot. Seconds later, he forced himself from the chair, reaching for the wall as he swayed. He had to escape. If they drugged him, and he confessed about Quinn, they'd both end up dead.

He jiggled the locked door, then searched for something to pry it open. Nothing in the room would help. The small table and chair were wooden but rickety and would never be strong enough to break the door.

Racking his brain, he rushed back to the chair, flipped it over and noticed a nail that had come loose. Summoning all his strength, he pried it out, then ran to the door and jimmied it open.

One of the guards stepped to the door, his weapon drawn. Luke took him by surprise with a karate maneuver, slammed the man's head against the wall until he passed out, then grabbed his gun. He glanced up and down the corridor, heard the sound of men's voices from the south end, and took off in the other direction. Three hallways down, he noticed a window and crashed through it. An alarm suddenly rent the air. The sound of men's bootsteps rushed toward him, guards' shouts echoing down the hall.

Luke jumped through the window, dropped to the ground and sprinted toward the woods where he'd entered the facility, his body throbbing, willing him to rest. But he fought the urge every step of the way. Behind him, the alarm wailed, guards rushed out and followed. Out of the corner of his eye, he saw men in uniforms jump into their jeeps.

Jesus, he didn't know if he'd make it out.

But Stella was back at the safe house waiting for him. He had to make sure she was safe. Find out if she'd slept with J.T. If she were responsible for his death.

Then what?

He had no idea. He had to focus on escaping now.

Adrenaline kicked in, and he sped up. But the guards

closed in on his tail. Just when he reached the edge of the woods, and he thought he might lose the men, shots rang out.

The first one pierced his lower back, sending a stinging pain down his leg. Another one grazed his shoulder as he fell to the ground and tried to claw his way into the woods.

STELLA CONTINUED studying the files, each time tidbits of the missions resurfacing, each time her distaste for what Sutton had turned her into sickening her. Why had she not been stronger? Able to fight his brainwashing techniques?

Because she owed her genetics to him?

A shudder rippled up her spine.

She fished through several more files, then found pictures of her with another man. She read the data. J.T. Osborne.

Dear heavens, Luke's partner.

She skimmed the material, her anxiety rising as she realized that she had been working with J.T. That J.T.'s death had ultimately led her to seek out Luke.

But was she responsible for J.T.'s demise?

Sutton's cell phone trilled, and he answered it, his jaw tightening as he listened. As he hung up, he turned to her with a smile. "You said you were here to stay now, Stella?"

She nodded, a mixture of disgust and fear welling in her throat.

"Then come with me. I know exactly how you can prove yourself."

Anxiety knotted her stomach at Kat's and Jaycee's

smiles. Wondering what Sutton had in store for her, she followed him to his Cadillac, her mind spinning. That call had something to do with her. And maybe with Luke.

Sutton remained quiet as his driver wound from the island to the marina. When she heard Sutton commandeer a boat for them to go to Nighthawk Island, the tension in her body doubled. Was he going to force her to undergo some kind of physical test? Drug her again?

Or perhaps he wanted to recondition her with some sensory deprivation treatment.

She trembled at the thought. She could not be locked up again. Deprived of light. Endure those shock treatments…

Salty water sprayed her, and the wind whipped her hair around her face as they zoomed across the choppy waters in the boat. Stella fought her nerves while formulating a plan in her head. If Sutton had sinister plans for her, she'd have to escape, find a phone, call Luke, warn him. She'd do anything just to see his face again.

When they reached the island, Sutton climbed ashore, then reached for her hand. Hers trembled. His felt icy to the touch.

He put his arm around her, guided her to a Jeep where a uniformed guard waited, an Uzi slung over his massive arm. She was sure Sutton was armed as well, leaving her feeling even more vulnerable. She wished she hadn't left the gun Luke had given her in the cabin, but she'd wanted to prove to Sutton she was playing his game.

She scanned the island, noted the palm trees, the woods and the sections of uninhabited land. The scenery would have been beautiful if not for the dire secrets the island held. Trying to remain calm, she glanced at Sutton, hoping for some sort of a commentary or announcement as to his plan, but he remained silent, his expression as granitelike as the concrete pillars that formed the guard towers protecting CIRP.

She forced herself to remember the night before. The way Luke had touched her. The way he'd held her. The way he'd moaned her name as he'd slid inside her.

She desperately wanted that feeling again.

The Jeep bounced over the ruts of the unpaved road, slinging seashells and dirt, closing the distance between her and whatever test the island held.

Another turn, and they stopped at a small building, one separated from the main facility. It was growing dark outside, the gray sky casting a dim murkiness over the building, adding to her frayed nerves. This building was separate for a reason.

So no one would know what was inside.

Maybe Sutton had decided to kill her...

"Come, Stella. I have something you need to see."

She accepted his outstretched hand, determined to play the part she'd commissioned for herself at his house.

The guard let them in, and Sutton walked her back to a small room with no windows. Shadows clung to the walls and ceiling, and the floor was made of cold concrete.

A body lay sprawled on the cement. Blood oozed into a puddle beside the man. His hair was dark... his size looked right. Dear God, no, it couldn't be.

Sutton stalked forward, then kicked the man, triggering more blood to spurt from his injuries. He grunted, then rolled over, and Stella's heart vaulted to her throat.

It was Luke.

He'd been shot twice, was unconscious and had been beaten so badly he looked near death.

"WHAT HAVE YOU DONE to him?" Stella asked.

"We need information." Sutton smirked. "He wasn't forthcoming."

Stella turned to Sutton, every cell in her body honed with hatred. For all he had done to her. For letting Nadine and Bianca die. For hurting Luke.

"What kind of information?" she said through gritted teeth.

"The name of the undercover agent here at Nighthawk Island." Sutton twisted a strand of her hair around his finger. "You want to save lover boy. Tell me, Stella."

"I told you I don't know."

"Ahh, he didn't trust you with that information?"

He was right. Although she couldn't blame Luke. It was better she didn't know.

Sutton moved to the counter along the wall, opened a drawer and removed a hypodermic. "If you really are working with me, then give him this."

Stella stared at the needle, her mind lapsing back years. To all the injections she'd been given. "What kind of drug is it?" Stella asked.

Luke moaned and opened his eyes, looking up at her. He had a dazed expression as if he was fighting for his life. She couldn't let him die.

"A truth serum," Sutton said.

"No," Luke groaned. "Deadly."

Sutton laughed. "The Tank simply told you that, Devlin. It is nothing but a truth serum." He offered Stella a challenging look. "Then again, he might be right."

Stella schooled her reaction. Sutton was forcing her to take the ultimate test. Whether the drug was deadly or not, Sutton would never let Luke go, not alive.

"Let him live, and I will work with you," Stella said coolly. "You can erase my memory."

Sutton's brow arched. "Devlin knows too much, Stella."

"You can erase his memory, too, Drake." She hardened her eyes. "Use your logic. If Luke walks away alive with nothing to pin on you, it will draw far less attention to you and CIRP than another murder."

Sutton stared into her eyes, seemingly studying her. Searching to see if she were bluffing.

"I'll swear my allegiance to you," Stella said. "I'll go willingly and never leave your organization again."

Sutton paused, his assessing look lingering for a tension filled minute. Then he shook his head. "Give him the shot, Stella. You must follow my commands now if I'm to believe you."

She offered Luke an apologetic look, then accepted the hypodermic from Sutton. Seconds later, she moved slowly toward Luke.

LUKE STRUGGLED to make sense of what was happening, but his head was foggy, his body shutting down. Riddled with pain, he lifted his head as Stella approached. If the drug held the deadly chemical the Tank had promised, his pain would grow intense quickly.

Then it would be over.

But what would happen to Stella?

He couldn't allow her to sacrifice herself to Sutton and be a pawn in his twisted game the rest of her life. Even if she had seduced and killed J.T…

She knelt and looked into his eyes. Tears misted her dark eyelashes as she lifted his arm and pushed at his sleeve. "I'm sorry, Luke."

"Shh." He forced a pain-filled smile. "The memory erasing would never have worked, Stella. I love you too much to ever forget you."

A tear trickled down her cheek, then another. "But, Luke, I've done so many bad things…. Your partner…"

He didn't want to hear her say it. He tried to lift his fingers to wipe away her tears, but his hand fell limp to his side.

"Go ahead, Stella," Sutton barked.

Stella closed her eyes, squeezed Luke's hand, then raised the needle.

Chapter Fourteen

Stella couldn't do it.

In spite of her suspicions about Luke's partner and her past, Luke had just confessed his love for her. And although she couldn't voice the sentiment herself, she knew in her heart that she loved him. But how could he ever forgive her for her past transgressions?

And what if she *had* killed his partner…? Her memories were still so scattered.

Sutton inched up beside her as if to take pleasure in watching her give Luke the injection while one of the guards hovered nearby. Thankfully the Tank and the second guard hadn't returned yet.

Sutton wanted her to betray Luke. Irate at the thought, Stella angled her head and smiled at him, then suddenly shot up, took him by surprise and jammed the needle into his thigh. The guard lurched forward, but she grabbed his gun and shot him, sending him down in a dead heap.

Sutton yelped, and clutched his leg as he collapsed onto the floor, his eyes bulging in shock. "What have you done, Stella?"

"I'd rather die with Luke than to go back and be the person you made me."

Sutton's body jerked. "No, Stella…"

"Now tell me the truth, Drake. What happened to Raul? He was helping me escape, I remember that much. So why would I have killed him?"

Sutton's breathing had grown erratic. Realizing his death was imminent, he mumbled, "I killed him. Had to get you back."

Stella narrowed her eyes. "Because I had fallen for Luke?"

He nodded. "You wanted out. I couldn't lose you."

"What about J.T.?" Stella asked.

Sutton groaned and rocked back and forth. "You were working with him. Leaking information from us to him…he had to die."

Stella gasped. So she hadn't killed him. Thank God.

"So you drugged Stella," Luke murmured slowly. "Then you framed her for Jarad's murder to force her to rely on you."

Sutton nodded. "It would have worked, too, if you hadn't shown up."

"What about her mother?" Luke asked in a low voice. "You abducted Stella and the others, didn't you?"

Stella glanced at Luke. He was growing weaker and weaker.

"Did she sell me?" Stella asked.

Sutton hesitated, his body spasming. The drug had been lethal. He was turning blue.

If she'd given it to Luke, he would be dying now.

He still might be. She had to get him immediate medical assistance.

Sutton gasped, then lapsed into a series of convulsions that robbed his reply.

Stella bent down to shake him. She wanted that answer. But Sutton's eyes rolled up in his head, and he gasped his last breath. Luke choked, coughing up blood, and there was no more time. She had to hurry or he would die here with Sutton.

She reached for Luke and slid her arm under his shoulder for support. "Come on, we have to get out of here."

"I can't make it," Luke groaned. "Go on, Stella, save yourself."

A tall dark-haired man with bulging muscles opened the door.

She didn't hesitate. She grabbed Sutton's weapon and fired a single bullet. A perfect shot. The man's body bounced backward and hit the wall, blood spurting from his forehead.

"I'm not leaving without you, Luke."

He waved her off. "Go on, you can make it faster on your own…" His voice broke off in pain.

"No, Luke." She wielded the gun beside her, grabbed the dead man's weapon, and dragged Luke to a standing position. Luke struggled, his body sagging as they ran toward the door.

As they crossed the hall, a guard jumped out from the corner and fired. Stella and Luke ducked into a doorway, then she slipped forward and pulled the trigger. The guard dropped to the floor. Together, she and Luke battled their way past two more guards to the outside. Darkness shielded them as they wove into the shadows along the side of the building. She spotted Sutton's Jeep, so she motioned to Luke, and they set out for it. Halfway there, another guard attacked, but Luke shot him while Stella climbed into the driver's seat and hot-wired the vehicle. Luke fell into the passenger's seat, ducking low, but covering them as another guard chased after them.

Stella hit the accelerator and tore down the graveled road toward the boat where she'd come onto the island.

"No, go the other way," Luke shouted over the wind. "There's a cove where I came in. I stashed a boat there. It's secluded, the security cameras won't pick us up."

She nodded, spun the Jeep onto the graveled road that led in the opposite direction, then hurled over rocks and ruts in the dirt as they wound their way across the island.

Stella glanced at him, her stomach lurching at his pallor. He needed medical treatment immediately. She yanked his phone from his pocket.

He punched in the numbers, his hands shaking. She pressed the gas and sped up. Checking over her shoulder, she noticed another Jeep in the distance behind her.

"Spencer, it's Devlin. I need backup. Get someone to meet me at the cove where I docked on the island."

Stella grabbed the phone. "And have an ambulance ready. Luke's been shot twice, he needs immediate medical attention."

Luke stared at her, his eyes bleak as they raced ahead through the darkness.

Stella prayed that they made it in time. She couldn't lose Luke now.

LUKE STRUGGLED to remain conscious, but his body was too weak. He'd lost a lot of blood, and the pain had dulled to a deep aching throb that warned him he might not survive. But at least Stella was safely away from Sutton.

He knew what that altercation had cost her. She'd killed the only man she'd ever thought of as a father. And she'd done it to save his life.

He closed his eyes, unable to fight the dizziness. He had to reserve his strength in case Stella needed him later. But Spencer was on his way, or maybe he'd send Black and Fox.

He blinked and glanced at Stella, amazed at her strength. No wonder he'd fallen in love with her. When he'd first met her, he'd glimpsed the vulnerable child inside, but also detected the courage and strength below the surface. That combination had been too heady to resist.

If only he could erase the cruelties she'd suffered at the hands of Sutton.

Once again, fatigue claimed him. When he opened his eyes, they'd reached the cove. Stella slung the Uzi over her shoulder, then jumped out and rushed to help him. Determined not to be a burden, he grabbed the other weapon, and hoisted himself out. But his knees buckled.

She slid an arm beneath his shoulder and encircled his waist. Seconds later, a boat raced up to the shore, and Spencer jumped off.

"Thank God," Luke muttered.

Stella stilled beside him, her face turning ashen. "Oh, my God, it's you."

Luke frowned, still clinging to her. "You've met?"

Stella gripped him tighter. "Yes, Luke. He works with Sutton. He's…the monster they call the Master."

Luke staggered in shock, as if he'd had the air knocked from his lungs. "No." But the minute he uttered the denial, Spencer lifted a gun and waved it toward them.

A second later, Luke recovered. His mind spun, piecing together all the unknown factors of the last few months. J.T.'s death. Spencer being antagonistic toward him. His reaction when Luke had announced he intended to marry Stella. "What's going on?" Luke asked.

"You got too close," Spencer said. "Both of you."

"I don't understand," Luke said, the sea beyond a hazy blur as he clung to life.

"But she does." Spencer gestured toward Stella.

"You were with Sutton years ago, the day of the fire," Stella said as if in a daze. "I remembered seeing another man waiting outside the burning building, but I couldn't make out his face."

"I thought you wouldn't remember," Spencer growled. "But when Osborne came to me and said you wanted away from Sutton, I knew I had to do something."

Pain knifed through Luke. "You killed J.T.?"

Spencer shrugged. "I couldn't let him discover the truth."

"That you were in charge of that experiment years ago," Stella said.

"What about Quinn?" Luke barked. "Have you revealed his assignment?"

Spencer laughed. "Are you kidding? I plan to use him to extract information on some of the projects."

Then he'd kill him.

"So that's how Sutton and his team have gotten away scot-free with everything they've done the past few years," Luke said.

Spencer sneered. "Everything was working fine until Stella contacted you, Devlin."

Until he'd fallen for her. And vice versa.

Luke clutched at his chest. "You bastard."

Spencer glared at Stella. "And Sutton, the damn man had to go soft on you, too. Even bailed you out of jail thinking he could bring you back into the organization."

"But it didn't work," Stella said.

Because she was strong, independent, Luke thought. She'd been fighting to escape long before he'd met her. And J.T. had lost his life helping her.

"Get in the boat," Spencer ordered.

Stella and Luke exchanged wary glances, then Stella helped him forward. As soon as Stella climbed in, Spencer appeared behind Luke and shoved the gun in his back. Luke was dying already.

He refused to let Spencer kill Stella.

Besides, he'd vowed to avenge J.T.'s death, and he owed it to J.T. to make Spencer pay.

He coughed, doubling over, then caught Spencer by surprise with a sharp jab to his midsection. His gun hand wavered, and Luke spun around and struggled to grab it. Both men dropped to the ground, fighting to secure the weapon. Luke tasted dirt and blood, but he managed to slam his fist into Spencer's face. Spencer spat at him, then angled the gun toward Luke, but Luke jerked it back toward his superior. The gun fired. Once. Twice.

A third time, and Spencer's head lolled back.

Luke collapsed onto the ground, beside him, fighting for air.

Stella leaped off the boat and dragged him on board,

then started the engine and gunned it. The last thing he remembered before he lost consciousness was seeing her wild hair blowing in the wind, tears streaming down her cheeks along with the salty spray as she promised him she'd get him to the hospital.

STELLA HATED HOSPITALS. Hated them with a passion. But she hadn't left Luke's side for the past forty-eight hours. Luke's condition had been touch and go, but Stella had remained steadfastly by his side, praying that he would survive. Detectives Black and Fox had visited, and she'd explained what had happened, half expecting them not to believe her. Yet. Black had almost been sympathetic, had squeezed her shoulder, reassured her that Devlin was tough and that he'd survive.

It was just a matter of time before the police took her back to jail. After all, she'd not only violated bail, she had killed Drake Sutton. And Luke's superior was dead as well. If Luke didn't wake soon and corroborate her story, they'd probably try to pin his superior's murder on her.

She couldn't go back to prison.

At least not until she found her mother. Stella had to know what had motivated her mother to sell her child.

And if both her parents' genes had been vile.

Luke stirred and groaned, and she reached for his hand, cradling it between her own. His was large, masculine, his fingers thick and swollen. But he had been so gentle when he'd made love to her that she still craved the feel of his hands on her body, arousing her, making her quiver with desire.

He slowly blinked open his eyes, his expression pained and weak. "How long have I been here?"

"Two days," she said, although it felt like an eternity. "I…Spencer?"

"He didn't make it," Stella said softly. "Detectives Black and Fox have stopped by several times. They want your version of what happened on the island."

He nodded. "Are you okay?"

She was numb. Scared of the future. Terrified of losing Luke, but parting was inevitable. "I'm a survivor."

"You're more than that, Stella, you're a gutsy, brave woman."

Luke cut his gaze sideways, a deep sadness darkening his eyes. "I can't believe Spencer killed J.T. and God, what he did to you." His breath caught. "I should have caught on sooner and destroyed him."

"I'm sorry, Luke." She squeezed his hand again. During the past forty-eight hours more of her memories had returned. "J.T. was a nice man. He tried to arrange for me to escape Sutton—" Her voice broke, guilt setting in. "But I didn't sleep with him, Luke. I swear, our relationship wasn't like that. He loved his wife." She paused. "In fact, his devotion to her was one of the things that made me realize how unhappy I was. That I wanted a real life. Someone to love." But she'd never thought it possible.

And she didn't deserve it. A good man was dead because of her. And Luke had almost died, too.

"His wife will be relieved to know that," Luke said.

"What about you?"

He nodded, his mouth pinched, although he didn't proclaim his love again.

"You had a lot of guts to betray Sutton and try to break the hold he had over you, Stella."

"Don't make me out as some hero," she whispered raggedly. "If I hadn't asked J.T. for help, he wouldn't be dead." *And you wouldn't be lying here near death yourself.*

"It's over," he said simply. "J.T. was doing his job. And I'm just glad we got Sutton and Spencer. Now J.T.'s wife and son can at least get their insurance settlement." He squeezed her hand. "What about you? Are you okay?"

She nodded, although for her, the haunting images from her past would never cease. J.T. and Raul had both died for her. And then there was that government official she'd murdered. Luke wouldn't be able to let that go.

And she couldn't blame him.

He sighed, looking exhausted, and she bent over and kissed him. "Rest now, Luke, you need it."

"Black?"

"I'll tell him you woke up. I'm sure he'll be in later."

Stella sat with him until he drifted back to sleep, then she gently kissed his cheek again and slipped out the door.

Before she turned herself in for her past crimes, she had to find her mother. Close the door on that part of her painful past *forever*.

STELLA HAD DISAPPEARED again.

Luke didn't know if he could handle losing her a second time.

"She's been gone a week now, Devlin," Detective Black said as he handed Luke a cup of coffee.

Luke had settled back into his cabin, although his body was sore, and he was moving slowly. Myra and her son had visited him twice already. She'd been thrilled to learn that J.T. had died an honorable death—he was a hero. He always would be in both their eyes.

She'd also confided that she'd started dating a coworker, but she was torn with guilt. Luke had assured her that J.T. would want her and their son to be happy.

"I'm worried about Stella," Luke admitted. "What kind of mental state she's in."

"She's a survivor," Black said.

But would she survive this time? Could she live with the guilt of her past? He hoped so. After all, none of it was her fault. She'd been brainwashed and traumatized. And no one had been there to protect her. Least of all Sutton, the man who should have taken care of her.

But Stella had a conscience, not like Kat or Jaycee. And those two were still missing, worrying him more. According to Black, they'd disappeared, taking Sutton's files with them. He wondered if they'd resurface and seek revenge against Stella, or if they'd use the opportunity to start new lives, far from the feds' scrutiny.

"She might not be safe," Luke said, voicing his thoughts.

"The police and our agents are looking for her. And from what I've seen, she can take care of herself."

Maybe physically, but not emotionally. Not all alone. She'd suffered too much.

His head throbbed as he contemplated where she might have gone. Then an idea dawned, and he knew he was on the right track. There was one more element in her past she still had to face.

"She's looking for her mother."

Black nodded. "That makes sense."

Luke grabbed the phone to make some calls while Black booted up Luke's laptop.

STELLA HAD FINALLY snuck into Sutton's place, although she hadn't been surprised to find that the feds had confiscated all his files and computers. Or perhaps Kat and Jaycee had taken them first.

She'd expected to find the two agents waiting for her at his compound, had looked over her shoulder for the past week to make certain they hadn't tracked her down to kill her, but they seemed to have disappeared. Maybe they were across the world on another mission, or lying low until the attention from Sutton's and Spencer's deaths died down.

Still confused over how she'd react if she actually located her mother, she pivoted to leave. Suddenly a figure appeared in the shadows.

She automatically reached for her gun.

But Luke inched out of the darkness, raising a warning hand. "You aren't going to shoot me, are you, Stella?"

She drank in the sight of him. Masculine, potent, so alive and sexy that her mouth watered. He seemed stiff, still impaired from his surgery and the two bullet wounds.

"You don't have to arrest me, Luke. I was going to turn myself in. Eventually."

His dark eyebrow slid up. "Is that a fact?"

"Yes." She sucked in a sharp breath and squared her shoulders, bracing herself for his reaction. "I read Sutton's file on me. I know I'm a killer."

He nodded. "So am I."

She swallowed at his unexpected response.

"I just wanted to find my mother before I had to go to prison," she said, hoping he didn't think she was making excuses.

"I know. I figured that out."

She frowned. "So you've been watching me?"

"I can't let you go, Stella. Not after all we've been through."

She held out her hands, bracing herself for the claustrophobia that would assault her as the handcuffs closed around her wrists. "I understand, Luke, you saved my life. I won't ask you to jeopardize your career for me any more than you already have."

"You saved my life, too." He gripped her hands in his, forgoing the cuffs, puzzling her more. "And for the record, you were worth jeopardizing my career for. Thanks to your help in getting Sutton, the bureau is dropping all charges against you. In fact, there is a job offer on the table."

"A job?"

"Yes, as an agent."

"The U.S. government wants me to work for them?"

He nodded. "With me if you like. You can be my new partner. Of course, they'll require you to undergo an evaluation and some therapy."

A hint of euphoria filled her at the thought. She'd planned to see a therapist already. Disappointment followed.

"What's wrong, Stella? You don't want to work with me?"

"It's not that, but Luke...I am Sutton's daughter. I have his genes."

Luke swallowed. "He lied to you, Stella. I've been doing some investigating. He's not your father."

"How can you be sure?"

"DNA. Besides, even if he was, genetics don't make a person. You chose to leave him, meaning even if you were related, you're your own person."

She contemplated his answer, then his job offer. "I don't want to be an agent anymore," she whispered.

He stepped toward her, his voice husky. "What *do* you want?"

To be with you.

She still couldn't voice her desires. She didn't deserve Luke. And she had to find her mother, confront her. She'd never be able to heal until she did.

He moved closer, until he was a mere heartbeat away. Until she inhaled his masculine scent and felt his touch as his finger caressed her cheek. Her body tingled in response, every nerve ending vibrating with need.

"How about my partner in life?" he murmured.

She clamped her bottom lip with her teeth. "You don't know what you're saying, Luke. I'm not a good person."

A fierce look crossed his face just before he dragged her to him. Their bodies touched, chest against chest, lips only an inch apart. "You're a strong, beautiful, wonderful woman. You survived unspeakable things and fought to escape a madman. That makes you special in my book."

"Luke—"

"You were willing to die beside me, Stella." His eyes raked over her, hungry, needy, possessive. "You may not have confessed your undying love for me, but you showed me. Completely."

Tears glistened in her eyes, blurring her vision. Her heart was aching. Her body begging for his. "I do love you, Luke."

"I love you, too, Stella. I always will." His breath brushed her cheek as he lowered his mouth and claimed hers. His kiss was commanding, but gentle, seeking, taking, giving. She relished the moment, and loved him back, accepting his tenderness and understanding.

"Luke...I still need to find my mother, confront her about selling me. I don't think I'll ever be whole until I do that."

"Shh, from now on, you're not alone. We'll find your mother together."

She nodded against his cheek, then they walked out of Sutton's compound hand in hand.

Later that night, as they lay in bed, their bodies entwined, their lips and souls touching, Stella reached inside her dresser and removed a heart-shaped candle.

"What's that?" Luke said with a smile.

"A symbol of my heart," Stella whispered. "Because it will burn for you forever, just as my body will."

He grinned and lowered his mouth to take her nipple between his teeth. His fingers traced a path down her naked belly, igniting the flames once again as he silently agreed to stoke the burning embers forever.

Epilogue

Stella had had the nightmares again. She was lying on the cot in the room with the other girls crying for her mother. She heard the soft whispers around her. The warnings that she had to forget. That her mother was never coming back. That she had to do as the big man with the dark eyes commanded, or she would end up dead.

But this time she woke in Luke's arms.

Safe. Loved. As his wife.

She sat upright, her heart pounding. This was the day she'd confront her mother about why she'd sold her into slavery years ago. And she'd tell her mother all the things they had done to her during her years with Sutton. Watch her reaction for any regrets.

Luke sat up, the covers sliding down to reveal his bare torso as he slipped his arms around her. "Nervous?"

She nodded. "I know I should have let it go. But I have to do this."

"I understand." He embraced her, his chest brushing hers. "No matter what happens today, Stella, I'll be there. It won't change anything between us."

She kissed him tenderly, so in love she thought she might burst. In fact, there were times the last few months when she'd almost given up the search. Told herself that her life with Luke was enough.

That and the precious baby growing inside her.

But Luke had pulled strings. He hadn't given up and had located her mother.

As if he'd read her thoughts, Luke lowered his head and kissed her belly, softly caressing her swollen abdomen as he did each night. They'd both wanted a baby right away, but had been worried about any lingering remnants of the drugs she'd been given by Sutton. Thankfully all the test results had proven clean, and now they had their first child on the way.

"I love you, Luke."

"I love you, too, Mrs. Devlin. And I can't wait to meet our son."

The baby kicked, and Luke grinned while she thought of the child inside her now. Once again, she wondered how any mother could abandon her own offspring, much less sell it to someone like Sutton.

"Come on, let's get this over with," Luke said. "Then I have a surprise for you."

Stella nodded, drawing strength from Luke, then quickly showered.

A half hour later, they drove to the small town of Moultrie, Georgia. She'd been shocked to learn that her mother had lived so close by all these years. And embittered to know that she'd never attempted to find Stella.

Luke drove through the small town, located the street named Pecan Drive, then came to a stop in front of a small, white, wooden house. Although the grass had turned brown, the yard was well-tended, a flower bed of pansies dotting the front with color. Stella sucked in a sharp breath at the sight of the woman who opened the screened door and walked out.

Her mother's name was Dorothy. She had been twenty-five when Stella was born, single, living alone, and had probably needed money. Although to Stella, nothing justified selling a child.

As Luke cut the engine, Stella memorized her features. Dorothy had classic features framed by a soft, blond bob that held touches of gray. Her petite frame resembled Stella's prepregnancy figure.

Stella's heart squeezed. Would Dorothy see the same similarities, or be upset that Stella had found her?

Luke squeezed her hand, and Stella offered a tentative smile. She reached for the car door, but he jumped out and met her, helping her out, always the protective, loving husband and doting father-to-be.

Dorothy descended the steps, slanting her hand over her eyes to see through the sun. "What can I do for you, folks?"

Stella studied her, glad they hadn't phoned ahead. She wanted the woman's gut response when she introduced herself.

Then the most miraculous thing occurred. Dorothy's eyes widened, and tears streamed down from her eyes. "Stella?" She walked toward Stella, her hands outstretched. "Oh, my God, is it you, baby? Is it really you? You're alive…after all this time."

Stella narrowed her eyes, and Luke nudged her forward. "Mom?"

"Oh, my heavens!" Dorothy covered her mouth with her hand and shrieked, then rushed toward her and crushed her in her arms, sobbing. "I thought whoever took you had killed you. But it's not true, you're here and alive."

Stella stiffened, confused at Dorothy's reaction, wanting so badly to believe that her mother really cared.

Dorothy slowly released her, but gripped Stella's hands. "The night you were kidnapped, I…I thought I would die. It was the worst day of my life." She smiled through her tears, then cupped Stella's face in her trembling hands. "I prayed every day that whoever stole you from me had taken care of you. That you were at least with a decent family, but my heart ached every day. And I prayed and prayed… And one day the police came and told me about this baby who had been found dead…it was unrecognizable. I thought it was you."

Tears swelled in Stella's eyes.

"I was kidnapped?"

"Yes, honey, at the park in Savannah where I met your father."

"What happened to him?" Stella asked.

"He died in an accident before you were born." Dorothy reached out and felt Stella's hair.

"What do you mean he died? What was his name?"

"Calvin," she said softly. "We were so in love. But a hit-and-run accident took his life."

"And you're certain he was my father?"

For a moment Dorothy's face flushed with irritation, then hurt. "Of course, I'm certain. He was the only man I was ever with." She paused, wrinkling her forehead. "If you don't believe me, I'll show you a copy of your birth certificate."

Stella hesitated. Dorothy had no reason to lie to her. But Sutton had—he'd wanted to cover his tracks.

"You kept it?"

"Of course." She hurried inside to a desk drawer and removed an envelope, then took out several pictures of her as a newborn, then as she'd grown. Stella's heart raced at the sight of her birth certificate.

"I can't believe you saved all those photos."

"Of course I did." Her voice cracked. "I…waited for years in Savannah, hoping they'd find you. Every day I'd look out the window and pretend you were coming home to me, But finally…" More tears rained down her face, and she choked. "Finally I gave up after that cop showed up. I had to move away. The agony of not knowing, of walking through the park every day and searching for you was killing me."

Stella heard the sincerity in her mother's voice and realized they had both been victims.

That her memory of her mother crying out for her was real…

That Sutton had lied to her about everything.

"I've been looking for you for a long time," Stella whispered thickly.

Her mother swiped at her tears as her gaze traveled over Stella. "I can't believe you're here now. I've missed so much time with you." A note of anger and bitterness hardened her voice. Then she brushed Stella's hair from her cheek as if she were a little girl. "You have to tell me where you've been. What happened. Have you been happy? Did someone adopt you? Did they give you a nice home?" Her voice broke again. "Oh, I hope they did, Stella. I…so worried about you being happy. I felt so helpless."

Stella glanced at Luke, the silent question fluttering between them. But she knew the answer. Her mother had obviously suffered enough already. She wouldn't inflict any more pain on her now.

Her life was so full of love there was no more room for bitterness or blame.

"I'll tell you everything later, Mom. Just not now." she said. "I just want to get to know you."

Tears overflowed from Dorothy's eyes again as she nodded. "Oh, honey, I'm so glad you're back. I was so angry that you were taken...."

Stella hugged her, savoring her warm welcome again, letting it wash away the fears and bad memories. Finally, when they pulled away, she remembered Luke.

"Mom, there's someone very special I want you to meet. My husband, Luke Devlin."

"Luke Devlin, what a nice name." Her mother tittered. "And what a handsome man."

"Luke's an FBI agent. He helped me search for you."

Her mother hugged Luke, wiping at her tears. "Thank you so much. I...never married, never had more children. I didn't think I could stand to lose anyone else I loved again."

"You won't," Stella whispered as she hooked her arm though her mother's. "In fact, we'll all be a family together."

HER REUNION was one of the most emotional moments of her life. She and Luke and her mother went inside for tea and laughed and talked. Finally Luke stood.

"I hate to cut this reunion short, but we have to go. I have a surprise for Stella."

Stella's mother smiled. "I think you've found a special man, Stella."

"You're welcome to come with us," Luke said. "In fact, I think you'd enjoy it."

Dorothy's hand trembled as she reached for Stella's. "Do you want me to come along, Stella?"

"Yes, please, Mom. I'm not ready to leave you again."

"Don't worry," her mother said. "I might have missed out on being your mother all these years, but I'm not going to miss anything about my grandbaby's life, or the rest of yours."

They laughed and followed Luke to the car. A half hour later, he parked at Detective Black's house.

Stella searched her husband's face, constantly amazed at him. "What's going on, Luke?"

He winked. "Come on, your surprise is inside."

She accepted his hand, trusting him more than she'd ever thought possible. When the door opened, Adam Black's wife, Sarah, greeted them. A chorus of "Surprise!" erupted around the room. All her new friends from Luke's office and the Savannah police department, were jammed inside, along with J.T.'s wife and son.

Stella gaped at the colorful balloons, streamers and the banner above the mantel congratulating her and Luke on the baby. Brightly wrapped presents were stacked on one table beside a cake decorated with pink-and-blue icing. A baby carriage sat in the corner with a big, yellow bow on the hood.

"This is wonderful," Stella whispered. "The best day of my life." She turned and kissed Luke. "Next to marrying you, of course."

He caressed her cheek, then ushered her inside. Stella hugged Sarah, then introduced her mother and the three of them went inside to enjoy the baby shower together, just as they would enjoy being together the rest of their lives.

Stella patted her growing tummy. Her world was finally complete. All the lies and pain and secrets were part of a past she was leaving behind.

Now she was sailing into a bright and beautiful future, complete with her mother, a wonderful husband who loved her, and a son to spoil and protect....

Prologue

Lisa Langley couldn't breathe.

Heat engulfed her, and perspiration trickled down her brow and neck, the cloying air filled with the scent of decay, blood and foul body odors.

Her captor's smell.

Her own.

She was suffocating. Being buried alive. Swallowed by the darkness.

Cold terror clutched her in its grip. The wooden box imprisoning her was so small her arms and legs touched the sides. An insect crawled along her chin, nipping at her skin, biting at the flesh. She tried to scream, but her throat was so dry and parched that the sound died.

Tears mingled with the sweat on her cheeks, streaming into her hair and down her neck. What kind of maniac buried a woman alive?

The same kind that robbed you of your life for the last few days.

William White. The man she'd dated off and on for the past six months.

How could she not have known what kind of monster he was?

She trembled as the terrifying memories rushed back—the first day the suspicions had crept into her mind. The subtle nuances that William possessed a violent streak. His morbid fascination with the articles in the papers describing the murders.

The odd look in his eyes when the press named him the Grave Digger.

Above her, a shovel scraped the ground. Dirt splattered the top of the box. Rocks and debris fell on top of her. The shovel again. More dirt. Over and over. The eerie drone of his voice humming an old hymn faded in and out as he worked.

The past few days had been a living nightmare. He'd heard her call the police. Had known she'd figured out his identity, that the FBI was coming for him.

There was nothing else he could do, he'd told her—except treat her as he had his other victims.

She'd thought each day she would die. But each time, when he'd finally left her, bruised and hurting, she'd managed to will herself to survive. Because she'd thought she might be rescued. That Agent Brad Booker would make good on his promise to protect her.

Particles of dirt pinged off of the mound above her again, the sound growing faint as she imagined him finishing her grave.

And then the silence.

It frightened her the most.

He had gone. Was never coming back. Her body convulsed with fear. She was hidden beneath the ground, locked in the endless quiet.

No one would ever find her.

She tried to raise her hand, to roll sideways so she

could push at the lid. Her right hand was broken, throbbing with pain, but she dragged her left one to her side, twisted enough to turn slightly, and clawed at the top. Her nails broke into jagged layers, and her fingers were bloody and raw, splinters jabbing her skin.

He had nailed the top shut. And laughed as she'd begged him to stop.

A few grains of sand sifted through the cracks, pelting her face. She blinked at the dust. Tasted dirt.

It was so dark. If only she had a light.

But night had fallen outside when he'd laid her in the casket.

She pushed and scraped until her fingers grew numb. In spite of the unbearable heat, chills cascaded through her as death closed in. Then slowly peace washed over her as she reconciled herself to the fact that she was going to die.

The life she'd dreamed about flashed in her mind. A beautiful white wedding dress. Getting married on a warm, sandy beach with the breeze fluttering the palm leaves, and the ocean lapping against the shore. Moonlight shimmering off the sand as they exchanged vows, while her father stood in the distance smiling proudly.

Then she and her husband were making love beneath the open trees. Promising to hold each other forever.

And later, a baby boy lay nestled in her arms. A little girl danced toward her.

A little girl. She could buy a birthstone ring for her just like Lisa's mother had for her. As she'd outgrown it, she'd made it into a necklace. But William had stolen that, too. Had ripped it from her throat and thrown it to the ground. It was lost forever. Just like her dreams.

Too weak to scream, the sob that erupted from her throat died in the dusty abyss of her prison.

The hopes of that life, of a family, faded as she closed her eyes and floated into the darkness.

SHE HAD to be alive.

The tires of Special Agent Brad Booker's sedan screeched on the wet asphalt as he veered onto the narrow dirt road leading around the old farmhouse. It was pitch dark, a cloudy, moonless night. He'd reached Death Valley.

Now he knew why it had been dubbed that gruesome name.

The grass and trees all looked brittle and frail from the drought, the outbuildings run-down and dilapidated, the lack of life a sign that it was deserted. He'd heard rumors about the area. That the soil wasn't fertile. That plants and animals couldn't thrive here. That families didn't, either.

He threw the car into park, jumped out, grabbed a flashlight and shovel from the trunk, and took off running. Behind him, two other cars raced up and parked. One, his partner Ethan Manning. The other, a squad car from the local Buford police.

His heart pounded as he tore through the dark, wooded area searching for fresh ground that had been turned. Limbs cracked and branches splintered beneath his boots. It had been over twenty minutes since Brad had received the call from the reporter.

The call describing the spot where Lisa Langley was buried.

Jesus.

Brad had promised to protect her.

But he'd failed.

Behind him, the men's voices sounded, each deciding which direction to go. It was so damn dark they could barely see their own feet, the towering oaks and pines like a jungle that drowned out any light. They parted, the locals with the police dogs allowing the hounds to lead. Brad wove behind them to the right, shone his flashlight over the dry ground, ignoring the buzz of insects and threat of snakes as he raced through the briars and bramble. A voice inside his head whispered to him that it was too late.

Just as it had been for the other four victims.

Another voice ordered him to fight the panic.

But the air in the box wouldn't last long—if the oppressive summer heat didn't cause Lisa to have a heatstroke first. And then the bugs would feast on her body.

He banished the image and forged on.

It seemed like hours, but only a few minutes passed. Then, one of the police tracking dogs suddenly howled.

"Over here!" the officer yelled. "I think we've got something."

Brad spun around and raced over toward him. Seconds later, he spotted the mound of dirt. The single white rose lying on top.

The Grave Digger's signature.

"Dammit!" His heart pounded painfully as he imagined Lisa Langley down below. Terrified. Dying.

Or dead already.

He loosened the knot in his tie, then jammed the shovel into the ground, swiping at the perspiration on his face with the back of his shirtsleeve. Manning and the locals followed, digging with frenzy. Dirt and rocks flew over their shoulders as they worked. Sweat poured down his face, the sound of the shovels and the men's labored breathing filling the humid air.

Finally, the shovel hit something hard. A wooden box. Just like the others.

His heart pounding, he dug faster, raking away the layers of soil until they uncovered the top of the box.

"Give me a crowbar and some light!" Brad shouted.

Ethan knelt beside him, shoved the tool into his hand. Brad attacked the box while the locals shone flashlights on the dark hole.

The wood broke and splintered. Brad clawed it open. His throat jammed with emotions. Fury. Rage. Guilt.

Lisa Langley. Such a beautiful young girl. Left naked and dirty. Bruised and beaten. Her fingers were bloody from trying to dig her way out. Her eyes were closed.

Her body so still.

"Too late," said one of the locals.

"Shit," the other one muttered.

"No!" Brad couldn't accept it.

Even though he never went to church—wasn't sure he was even a believer—a prayer rolled through his head as he reached inside and lifted her out. She was so limp. Heavy. Cold. He spread her across his lap, then immediately began CPR.

Ethan ran to the car and brought back blankets, draped them across her body, then felt for a pulse.

The two men's gazes locked. Paralyzed for just a second.

Brad continued CPR, muttering under his breath.

"Come on, dammit, Lisa, breathe! Don't you dare die on me."

Time lapsed into an eternity as they waited. Finally her chest rose slightly.

Ethan made a choked sound. "Jesus Christ, she's alive." He jumped into motion, punching in his cell phone. "Where the hell's that ambulance? Get it here ASAP—our vic is breathing!"

Brad sent a thank-you to heaven, then lowered his head and wrapped the blankets more securely around her, rocking her back and forth. "Come on, Lisa, stay with me, sweetheart," he whispered. "Help is on the way." He shook her face gently, trying to rouse her into consciousness, but she was in shock. He wrapped the blankets tighter, hugging her closer to warm her. Somehow, if she lived, he'd make it all up to her.

And when he found the bastard who'd done this to her, he'd make him pay with his life.

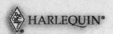

HARLEQUIN®
INTRIGUE®

Don't miss this first title in Lori L. Harris's exciting new Harlequin Intrigue series—

THE BLADE BROTHERS OF COUGAR COUNTY

TARGETED

(Harlequin Intrigue #901)

BY **LORI L. HARRIS**

On sale February 2006

Alec Blade and Katie Carroll think they can start fresh in Cougar County. Each hopes to bury the unresolved events of their violent pasts. But they soon learn just how mistaken they are when a faceless menace reappears in their lives. Suddenly it isn't a matter of outrunning the past. Now they have to survive long enough to have a future.

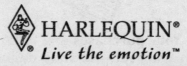

HARLEQUIN®
Live the emotion™

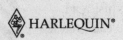

® HARLEQUIN®

INTRIGUE®

COMING NEXT MONTH

#897 CRIME SCENE AT CARDWELL RANCH
by B.J. Daniels
Montana Mystique
Former lovers reunite to dig up their families' torrid pasts and reveal the secret behind the skeleton found in an old dry well.

#898 SEARCH AND SEIZURE by Julie Miller
The Precinct
Kansas City D.A. Dwight Powers is a street-savvy soldier in a suit and tie. His latest case: saving the life of a woman caught up in an illegal adoption ring.

#899 LULLABIES AND LIES by Mallory Kane
Ultimate Agents
Agent Griffin Stone is a man that doesn't believe in happily ever after. Will private eye Sunny Loveless be able to change his mind?

#900 STONEVIEW ESTATE by Leona Karr
Eclipse
A young detective investigates the murderous history of a hundred-year-old mansion and unearths love amidst its treacherous and deceitful guests.

#901 TARGETED by Lori L. Harris
The Blade Brothers of Cougar County
Profiler Alec Blade must delve into the secrets of his past if he is to save the woman of his future.

#902 ROGUE SOLDIER by Dana Marton
When Mike McNair's former flame is kidnapped, he goes AWOL to brave bears, wolves and gunrunners in the Alaskan arctic cold.

www.eHarlequin.com

HICNM0106